Footprint Of A Ghost

By

Annabel Gallagher

Thank you

Sarah

Other books by Annabel Gallagher

Shadows in the Dark
Kiss of Fire

FOOTPRINTS
OF A
GHOST

CHAPTER ONE

I know who killed me, they say you don't know, that when you die you don't remember why or how. That if you don't know who killed you when you're alive, you won't know when you die, but it is not true.

I died violently and I didn't know my killer. I knew his face but not who he was, but the second I took my last breath, I knew who had killed me and why they had killed me. I think it would have been better if the books and films got it right, sometimes not knowing is better.

Watching yourself being killed, then seeing why in the eyes of the killer doesn't really help ones mental state, and knowing you can't do anything about it.

I mean have you tried to tell someone who you know, that you know who had killed you and why? Only to find you're talking to thin air, because that person can't see or hear you, it's not nice.

I tried killing my killer once, he was going to kill this other girl, turns out my killer is a serial killer, and a good one at that. He hasn't got caught and as far as I can tell: since I was killed he's killed about twenty five girls that I'm sure of.

I watched him as he buried their bodies; he has a body dump site where we all are. So you'd think that this place would be overrun with ghost's right? Wrong.

I'm the only one here truth be told, I haven't seen any other ghosts, where they all went, where they died I haven't a clue. I mean, I seem to be the only one who stuck around, they all seem to disappear after their deaths, I tried that, but nope, nothing worked.

I tried to follow the light like everyone says appears, you know don't walk into the light. But it turned out my light was a car driving down the road at night, had I been alive I would have been run over by the time I figured that one out. As I was still standing there the car would have hit me if it hadn't gone through me.

Getting back to my killer, I followed him out of the house, it turns out he is a copper!

Can you believe it, he got to the kidnapping spot first and cleans away anything he's missed, say a shoe has been left and his car has blood specks, then by the time someone else turns up, there is nothing there to show when that girl went missing, that made me feel sick, I can tell you.

I did try to stop him, but he went right through me, I'm a bit slow like that but anger makes me see red understandable right?

I mean I'm only 25, had my whole life ahead of me and this man decides to kill me, and this is the best bit, because I have blonde hair and brown eyes, he's mad because his girlfriend dumped him and moved country . I mean can you blame her?
So he decided to take it out on all the blonde hair brown eyes type in revenge. I mean, the last two victims of his weren't even real blonde haired girls! One had her hair dyed and the other was wearing a wig, he was pretty pissed at that last girl. Luckily she left her body before he had finished with it, I had to go outside I couldn't watch that because it bought back too many memories.
I did wonder why no one was looking for us, but he was clever you see; he only took those who were not missed: runaways and street walkers. I'm being polite here, but he spends time in the places he took them from, from what I have seen he sometimes follows them or with the street girls he talks to them makes friends and then wham they disappear and his all I will find out what happened to her and I will get justice. Sometimes he messed up and took someone like me, someone who would be missed he panicked over a girl once because her family like mind haunted the police to do something but he always made sure that there were no clues or evidence so that the investigation into what happened to us went nowhere, I was sure he took anything which might have looked like a

lead and lost it in the system although I have never caught him, he made it so nobody could prove any of us girls were missing: right!

So here I was stuck with nothing to do and nowhere to go, I fade in and out, sometimes I didn't know I did it but the weather would change the nights got longer or shorter and his hair style would change, he was always changing his appearance I was sure it was in case someone saw him clean shaven then beard, glasses no glasses, always different.

Watching my killer walking around free, that was the hard part the never changing nightmare girl after girl all dumped and forgotten but not by me never by me.

Little was I to know, things would change with his next victim, see one thing I learned was, never piss of a Reaper, as those guys have anger issues. Crazy right! I mean who knew?

I was sitting minding my own business and by that I mean I was sitting next to my corpse I wasn't looking my best, but then none of us were, I was glad that I couldn't smell because judging by the flies we were kind of ripe.

How he had managed to stop animals from eating us I would never know but nothing came to unearth us or investigate the smell, I heard a fox once but it yelped in pain when it got near I went to look but it was gone by the time I got there and I couldn't find anything to say why it stopped.

I knew we were deep in the country the road was along walk I had done it once out of boredom and I wondered what if one of us had managed to escape but that would be the wrong place to run for.

The forest we were buried in was at the back of his house, you could see the trees from the back but there was a field before you got to it.

I think at one time horses were kept there but not anymore it was kept empty now but he did cut the grass. I was guessing so he could see to the trees knowing we were there.

But back to me I was hidden in a group of trees half buried in the ground. He hadn't even bothered to cover me up properly, mind you I didn't think it had been personal as the other girls weren't buried completely as well, so I was guessing it was a thing for him to do we were all kind of scattered not piled but in a sort of circle I guess some of us were more buried then other.

The others weren't complaining being that they weren't around to see how their bodies had been dumped.

Suddenly I felt a tug which I have to say was something new, closing my eyes I opened them to find I was back in the room where I died in, I was watching from the corner of the room which was darker and damper than I remembered, I didn't like being there even thought I was dead it didn't change how I felt; it just made me feel helpless as there was nothing I could do.

So I stood ready, once again as a silent witness to another girl's murder and I guess I will stay there until he is caught as I am the only witness to all of this.

I looked around the chamber of horror, it was just a small room, I hadn't known this until I died, there was nothing special, just a small back room down some steps in a normal house where anyone could stay there was nothing to show the horror which went on inside, that was hard to swallow most of all.

The fact it looked so normal outside and inside right up until you entered this room. I stood still, the fear of him seeing me still racing through me each time.

I know stupid right, until you look into the face of your killer, don't judge, it made me mad that he had the power to do that to me, even in death I had no peace from him.

I swallowed the rage growing inside of me and looked up in time to see the next girl falling down into the room. He loved to push us knowing that he had tied our feet so we would fall, he would them laugh and walk away.

I listened for the slamming of the door and waited for the lights to come on, he like to throw us down in the dark and then ten minutes of trying to find out where you are and what was happening he would turn the light on and watch from a monitor.

I found that out the second time I watched him with a girl the first time was too hard for me to watch. He would leave us tied up with the light on so we could look around; he made sure we saw the dead things he had left all around us.

They were mainly arms or bits of hands, he got off on it, I had watched him once he had been laughing as the poor girl was screaming, he would then turn the light off again, and so the torture would start always the mental side first then the body.

I had stopped looking at them about the fourth day and pretended that they were props from a show.

It was the only way I could stop myself from losing my mind and the only way I could make myself go back into the room.

I had gone to the police station once to see if me or any of the other girls had been listed, but I found only two of us were being looked for me and the other girl I mentioned before.

I was down as a person and suspected foul play involved and the other girl was noted missing, but the family were certain enough that they had got her, like me on the homicide list.

The same cop was looking into us but the other girls were unnoticed that made me sad, he was killing us and no one missed them, that had been when I had decided to stand for them.

I went back several times to see how the investigation was getting on, I named the copper in charge "My Cop" but there was nothing for him to do, but he didn't give up he kept digging, my killer had done to good of a job of covering his tracks to leave anything but I kept hoping and kept checking.

I watched from the corner wondering what had brought me here the dark was not a problem for me anymore, I could see the cobwebs hanging around the place as I waited the small door open and waited for the next victim to come through.

Only this time it was different it was still a girl, he threw her down and he turned the light on straight away, I couldn't help myself even knowing it was no good I spoke.

"Close your eyes don't look."

I told her, I felt sick and panicky as I walked over to where she laid.

I was sure I was having a heart attack and had to remind myself I was dead. I had to do that a lot, you would think the message would sink in, but nope at least once a day I reminded myself.

I needed to touch her so badly, my hands shock and I screamed in frustration when my hand went through hers.

I found myself pleading with her, I didn't know why.

"Don't look baby please, don't look just shut your eyes."

To my shock she did as I said and closed her eyes shut she stayed still shaking on the floor.

"Its ok baby I'm here"

I whispered to her I could see she wanted to get up, but her hand was about to touch down on one of the other girls hands which had been left, so I told her to freeze, she did, that kind of freaked me out a little.

It's one thing to have hope that someone heard you but another when it happens, I was so used to no one taking any notice of me the shock was knocking me off my game.

Along with this need to help and to protect her the help I was used to but the need to protect, that was new.

I moved a little closer to her, I tried to get a look at her face but she was bent down and she had long hair covering the front.

"Can I move?"

I was so startled by her voice I jumped, glad she didn't see me. I looked around for where she could move to where there was a body part free, for some reason I really didn't want her seeing what had happened here, I cleared my throat and answered her.

"Yes, move back though and turn around open your eyes slowly."

Moving closer to her, I watched as she did as I said I couldn't really see her face as it was covered by her long blonde hair, well calling it blonde was a bit much as it was a dirty brown tangled mess at the moment.

But I was guessing it was some type of blonde, going by myself and the other girls he had brought here.

The fear riding me, the truth was creeping up on me and I knew, I didn't want to face it. Then I didn't have a choice to my horror she pushed her hair out of her face and I knew if I had still been alive I would have lost whatever had been in my stomach, the answer to my fear was staring me in the face.

Her hair would be white blonde, beautifully long and straight, for there sat my baby sister.

He had taken my sister and my mum and dad were going to lose the only child they had left to the same killer.

I didn't know how long I had been dead for, the dreaming in and out played with time it could have been two days or months.

I think it was more like two years judging by the amount of girls I had seen coming and going and the changes in "My Cop" when I went to the station not that anything in the investigation changed our faces were still there, so I guess not that.

If ghosts could cry I was sure I could fill a river. My cruel evil killer had my sweet, loving baby sister and he was going to hurt and kill her and there was nothing I was going to be able to do.

CHAPER TWO

"Hello?"

"Where are you?"

Her small sweet voice I hadn't heard properly till now, asked me and I wondered why I hadn't recognised it before and I knew that I had, that was why I had felt the way I had.

My brain had tried to shut it out, because I knew that voice as well as I knew my own.

"I'm by the window."

I answered her knowing she wouldn't be able to see me, as the window was boarded up and dark I knew she wouldn't have seen me, even if I was alive.

"Your voice, I know your voice, but it can't be you sound... you sound like my sister."

My heart broke at the quiver of her voice and the hesitation in her tone, I didn't know what to say, I mean what do I say, yes I'm your sister, yes I'm dead, but I'm talking to you or do I lie and tell her something else.

"I don't feel too good, where am I?"

I grasped the change of subject,

"What do you remember?"

I watched her struggle to sit up, wishing I could help her she managed to half sit before stopping, her cloths were dirty and covered in twigs and leaves, but she was dressed as if she had been at work.

She worked in a lawyer's office, she was an intern a good one too, She had just started but held such promise.

I smiled for a second at the memory of her dancing around the kitchen singing I'm going to be a lawyer at the top of her voice when she received the internship she was only twenty, very intelligent for her age but all to soon I felt the smile die, as I let the reality back in slowly, it felt as if the light in the world had gone out I didn't think I was going to be able to carry on, for a second the pain so great I took gulps of breaths I didn't need trying to calm myself, I watched her and noticed her skirt was ripped and her top stained, She wasn't going to like that she always kept her cloths clean changing if there was a small mark anywhere.

As she lifted her hand to her head I could see she had a bump and a cut on top of her right brow he had hit her hard, there was dried blood on the side of her face and her hair was matted with it turning the dirt brown a black colour instead of the light blonde.

"I had gone to talk to my sister at her grave, I know she's not there that she could still be alive it's not even a grave but a small tree we had found together.

When we had gone to visit our granddad at the church cemetery, nobody knows about it but I felt close to her there.

As if she could hear me. As I was walking back to my car someone stopped me and asked where the office for the cemetery was.
She stopped talking but I was glad the guilt I felt was choking me, she had gone to our tree and he had seen her there.
She had been taken because of me.
"I'm sorry "
"How long has your sister been gone?"
I asked, knowing I needed some time line to work with. I was shocked at the answer.
"Two years yet it seems like yesterday."
She answered
"You sound so much like her."
She whispered
I noticed her lips were cracked and chapped as she talked looking around I tried to see if he had left her any water, sometimes he did other times he didn't, each guest of his was different.
I couldn't think of them and me as victims anymore to think of my sister as a victim was too much for me, the rage had nowhere to go.
I stood watching her, there wasn't any water and there was nothing I could do, he had drugged her.
I knew from watching the others soon she would be sleeping, he wanted the drugs out of their system the first time he hurt them, us.
He wanted us to feel the pain, god the pain it had hurt.

I knew if I could cry there would be tears running down my face at what my sister was going to go through.

Looking up I don't know why habit, I think, is the only answer I could give, I did something I hadn't done since I died, I asked for help, I mean it couldn't hurt right I was dead so the great mystery of life should be clear to me.

It wasn't, I was still as clueless as everyone else about death.

Only the problem was I was dead!

So I guessed if there was someone, me praying to them I would be able to hear them answer right? But nothing happened, no voice spoke to me no amazing thing happened.

Looking down nothing happened and I stood helpless as my sister fell into any easy drugged filled sleep.

Turning to leave I needed out of this room for a while.

I was going to need to find some type of courage to stay with my sister, while he was there I was not going to let her go through it alone like I did, I heard the sound of wings rustling I turned again expecting a bird of some kind, I didn't care what kind of bird if a bird got in my sister could get out!

But to my disappointment and shock it wasn't a bird but a man.

I looked behind him but the window stayed covered and there was no other entrance he was not looking at me but at my sister.

"Who are you?"

I had to ask even knowing he wasn't going to answer or see me, but then he should be there himself so I guessed I might as well ask. For a second he looked up in my direction.

"A friend."

Yeah that made me feel better not! Yet someone else who could see and hear me it was making me feel a bit dizzy, I had gone two years with no one talking to me or seeing me, now in less than ten minutes I had two people seeing or talking to me, But he was different I could tell by the air in the room, it was like it was charged it reminded of me of the air before a storm you could almost feel it, But the room was cold and turning colder, I knew he hadn't walked into the room he had just appeared there was no other way of getting in and out of the room but for the door I had checked every bit of the room and had found nothing and that door hadn't opened.

I wondered if he was a ghost like me. But then why would he come here? The Killer never took men or boys and there was nothing to show that he ever had and I had been to his dump site, there were no males there.

Throwing that thought away as soon as it formed I knew he wasn't a ghost there was too much energy coming from him, he was too alive somehow and the cold he seemed to leak cold someone alive wouldn't be able to do that and live but even with the clear eye sight I had in the dark I couldn't see him clearly.

He kept to the shadows, I could see well enough to know he was there and he was looking at my sister again, but not well enough to see his face or what he was wearing the dark seemed to move with him keeping him hidden.

I moved a little in the dark but it was enough to bring his eyes and attention back to me, he crouched his hands going behind him but as he was lost in the dark I couldn't see what he was holding or doing he was fast and seemed as if ready for an attack.

His eyes I could see clearly they seemed to reflect silver light as he half stood half crouched into the shadows; I decided I needed to keep him from my sister he was dangers so I asked again.

"What do you want?"

I watched him as he crocked his head to one side and studied me as he once again straightened, his full attention hit me and I felt something moving around inside me.

I now know how it felt to be a mouse caught in a trap, fear caused through me and I was very glad that I was dead.

I didn't move as he looked, I found I couldn't I was unable to move, He was doing something which stopped me from looking away.

"Interesting," he muttered before he again turned around to stare at my sleeping sister, releasing me from what had kept me still.

"You seem very protective and angry, both are about this girl. It interest's me, what is it about this child, what do you think you can do to help her?"

I watched as he lifted his head more into the light that was when I noticed the fangs, please don't let him be a vampire, I prayed it was bad enough I had to somehow stop a serial killer from killing my sister, protecting her from a vampire as well might be a little too much not to mention the thought that vampires were real and there was no way I could become one was bad enough.

He sniffed the air with a half-smile on his face as if he had caught my thoughts.

"Ah yes that's it."

He pinned me with his eyes again, His face once again disappearing into the shadows.

"She's related to you"

He again crocked his head it reminded me of a predator watching its prey.

"Sister?"

Slowly I nodded my head the feeling that I had to answer him over powering my need to protect her. I didn't like the feeling and the second I was free from his eyes, I turned and left the room hoping he would follow me; to my fear and relieve he did.

We walked slowly through the house I noticed he was like me, moving through walls and doors, as if they weren't there so he must be some type of ghost but I had the feeling that wasn't it, I was missing something.

I stopped at the bedroom where the cop slept in a nice comfy bed while my sister slept on a dirt muddy filled floors.

Day light streamed through a gap in the curtains. He was a night cop, so I guessed that was why he slept during the day. I was about to move from the room when I got my first good look at the male with me and caught my breathe he was handsome his face was breath taking even with the fangs his eyes were pure silver and he had jet black hair, which fell over his forehead, but that wasn't what had me staring he was bare footed with only black ripped jeans on and wings of jet black stretched out behind him rising above his head and fulling down to his feet.

"Are you an angel come to take me?"

I couldn't help but ask I didn't want to go. Wouldn't go, till I helped my sister or she joined me. I wouldn't leave her alone not even for this angel!

But he smiled.

He answered me,

"No. I am just a friend."

I turned and walked through the house the kitchen was a bright cheerful place the walls yellow and bright I wanted to paint them black to show that this wasn't a cheerful place but a dark hell hole I walked through the back door to the outside, knowing I wouldn't feel the wind, but needing the impression of the sun on my face to help me escape the shadows if only for a little while.

I watched as he walked behind me a few seconds later and I have to admit it surprised me I had the feeling he wasn't used to following but to leading, I wondered if that was how he had died bare foot and only jeans maybe he had been leaving someone's bed and got caught by their other half? Again I caught a half smile on his face as if he was reading my thoughts and found me funny.

"You have two days to save your sister, after that you will walk into the light or I will have to take you."

He spoke and made me jump.

"Why? "

I asked him pushing away how his voice made me feel it was deep and gravely as if he had damaged his voice but it sounded so hot! No I pushed that thought away.

How the hell was I going to save my sister in two days?

And who was he to tell me I only had two days left!
I had been here two years and now he showed up telling me two days he could go to hell.

"Two days you shouldn't have been here this long but his killing so quickly you slipped through the cracks."

As I listened to his answers I straightened my shoulders before facing him head on.

Swallowing my fear I answered him.

"I will not leave my sister, who do you think you are to come here and telling me two days!
Go away."

I knew if I was alive I would never had stood up to him, but this was important to me so I needed to stand up to this vampire thing of a guy who had come straight out of my dreams, but boy, was it hard and judging by the look on his face he wasn't happy with my answering him.

He disappeared in front of me and I felt him reappearing behind me Clouds formed in the sky dark grey and black they rolled across the blue skies out of nowhere swallowing the sky up lighting struck in them forking through the clouds and an ice cold wind blew around us kicking leaves and things flying then as quick as it began it was gone the blue skies returning as quick as they had disappeared.

As I stood still to my surprise I felt his breath on my neck ice cold but burning hot at the same time before I heard his words then as I stood there digesting what he had said he vanished.

"I will tell you I am the grim reaper and you; I will eat if you disobey."

Some friend!

CHAPTER THREE

I stood there after he disappeared not sure what to do, the grim reaper! That I hadn't seen coming, hell if the grim reaper looked like that why the hell were the pictures of him with a cloak and a scythe?

There again if he didn't wear the cloak, I was guessing he would be mobbed and girls would be killing themselves just to get a look at him, yeah better he kept the cloak.

Which begged the question where the hell was his cloak?

Looking around me trying to think of something that would help me I felt him return.

The energy crackled around me as if I could touch it and I felt the cold this time before I saw him.

"By the way don't you have a dog?"

I turned to him

"Yes?"

"Just a thought."

He saluted me and again was gone.

A dog? What the hell? I started to walk back in to the house when it hit me, what he was trying to tell me dogs!

Of course!! Dogs and cats were known to see ghosts, I was so stupid, I should have thought of that myself!

Hesitating, I looked towards the house then up at the sun, seeing it I wish I could once again feel the rays of its heat against my skin.

You have no idea how much we take that for granted the heat, the touch of its warmth against your skin.

I wasn't cold or anything but I missed the feel of it the knowing I was alive.

The sun was high in the sky so I guessed it was about noon, see the problem with being dead was you didn't need time any more, I would close my eyes and when I opened them hours or days were gone.

I hadn't cared as I drifted along but now I had a clock ticking back in my life, time meant something again and it was ticking down.

I had time to see if my sister was still sleeping or not I closed my eyes and opened them in the room again.

She wasn't sleeping she was staring at the dirty wall in front of her, she was laying on her side the skirt she had on was all tangled up, but as she was tired up she couldn't do anything about it nor could I.

I could see from her swollen wrists she had tried to escape the cuffs she had on, they were red and swollen from her rubbing them and pulling at them her legs were better but only because she saw that the tights had held in place so they were red but

not bleeding yet she wouldn't be able to get free.
They were police issued so they were tough to
brake, well they need to be didn't they, given what
job they were used to do.
I walked up to her closer and knowing it was
hopeless I spoke anyway.
"Don't keep trying the cuffs they won't break."
I told her, but she didn't listen and went back to
pulling and twisting her wrists till they were
bleeding she didn't need to lose more blood.
"Stop."
I told her but again she didn't even acknowledge I
was there, moving closer I called her.
"Violet?"
She didn't even look up, she couldn't hear me
anymore whatever had made her hear me didn't
work now.
Once again I was just a ghost who no one could
hear and now my sister would think she was on her
own, Her hair was just one mass f knots I remember
how that had felt tight and tangled I had though, if I
ever get out of here I would cut my hair short but I
hadn't.
 I had died there with my hair tight and tangled, for
some reason once I died it wasn't a mess any more
it lay straight and long I could run my fingers
through it, but I didn't know if it was still dirty I
couldn't see myself in a mirror and I had no one to
ask, I was guessing it was clean it felt clean I could

touch myself and feel myself but nothing else everything my hand passed right through.
Shaking the memory I turned whispering,
"I'll be back."
But she didn't notice, that hurt more than when they couldn't hear me to have someone hear then not hear was the worse type of pain.
I willed myself to the killer and saw he was still sleeping he looked nice and comfortable laying on a fresh clean bed, looking around his room it didn't look as if it belonged to a monster it was clean and neat looking, but the colours were soft and relaxing not the sort you would think a monster would have. The wardrobe and Chester drawers were a light brown there was no cloths or rubbish on the floor his curtains were black and kept the light out of the room letting him sleep in the day or night without the light getting in. I could see where he kept the key to my sister prison if I could touch I would have grabbed it and ran but I couldn't his gun was by his bed side teasing me at how close it was.
I wanted to screech in his face and hit him again and again till he let my sister go.
He should be living in a hole a disgusting room at least something which say don't trust or there is something wrong with me, but there wasn't and he slept on and I knew he would stay that way till night.

So shaking my head I looked at his clock I had time before he came for my sister most of the time he gave them enough drugs to keep them sleeping while he slept but each girl had been different, sometimes he would give them only enough for a few hours.

I wondered sometimes if it was a test for himself another kind of game if they woke up early would they be able to escape or not, but most of the time he had broken something anyway, like an arm or leg, so it wouldn't make much difference if they had got the cuffs off or lay there awake for hours knowing that no one was going to come.

I remembered he had broken both of my leg, so I couldn't walk, the pain almost stopped me from trying to get free, I remembered that time as if I was there again the pain was all consuming and a long with it was a long burning in my arms and shoulders where my hands were cuffed, my hands would go to sleep and I would have pins and needles when I moved sometimes I would use the pain to try and fight the drugs hoping that I could clear my head long enough to think of a way to free myself but I never had.

Others he had tied up, he had cut another's feet off so she couldn't walk anywhere,

I shuddered at that memory; each girl had had it bad he enjoyed their pain.

No way was my sister going through that.

I closed my eyes and pictured my sister's room I didn't want to go to my room it hurt too much.

My mum and dad may have cleared my room as far as I knew, I had only been back at the house once and that had been at my mock funeral it hurt too much so I hadn't stayed for long.

Travelling as a ghost was easy you just closed your eyes and willed yourself where ever you wanted to go open your eyes and your there.

I opened my eyes and I was in my sisters room I stood there shock and sadness hitting me in waves her room was how she always left it tidy and neat but her bed was unmade it was as if she had just stepped out, I had to wonder just how long my sister had been gone, was it days or hours did they know or were yet unawares she was missing? If she had said she was working late then mum and dad may not be missing her yet, that mad man could have my sister and no one would know.

Was that what had happened with me, how long did he have me before my mum and dad knew I was gone? That I wouldn't be back, did they know up until they found my blood and cloths? Did they miss me? Were they looking for me still? Were they now looking for my sister? I knew I needed to leave her room to find out the answers but I stood in the room willing my feet to walk yet I didn't move, my eyes were drinking in my sisters life the one I had missed while being dead and I hit me I had been dead a long time.

I thought her room had been redecorated and changed from what I remember, it was older somehow.

There was a picture of us together next to her bed, it was one taken a few days before he had took me we were smiling at something out of camera shot, but we looked happy.

We had been happy till he had come into my life and ended it, shaking my head I walked through the closed door right passed my bedroom or where my bedroom should be I was too much of a coward to walk In and see what had happened to my room so I avoided it.

Walking down the stairs I could hear voices coming from the kitchen I followed them and stopped dead.

I saw my mum sitting at the table with dad standing next to her was a cop I didn't recognize was sitting at the table with them, she was small and had a police uniform on so I was guessing she didn't belong to the investigation, but was there to just hold my mum and dads hand at that time meaning that question one answered yes they knew my sister was missing.

I got distracted by my mum as I looked closer at her mums hair which had been jet black last time I saw her was now white and there were lines on her

face, I had never seen look like that she looked years older and her eyes were full of sadness.
I wondered how much of my death was the reason or how much of my sisters missing was.
The lines looked old as if they had settled in somehow so I was guessing since my disappearance and my dad didn't look any better, his hair was grey and he looked so tried they looked as if they had aged a hundred years since I saw them last.
Looking round the living room I notice picture of as all there were more than when I left more photos of me some were new and showed I was right my mum had aged after I went missing, there were pictures of mum and Violet and mums hair was grey there, dad looked tired but not as bad as he looked now, turning back I moved closer to listen as my mum talked.
"I want my girls found. Don't sit there telling me that my baby is dead you have no body you have nothing."
I smiled go mum, you tell him, Violet is still alive don't give up. But then she carried on
"My baby has been missing for two years now detective she isn't dead till I see her body Scarlet wouldn't just leave us and now Violet is missing.
No she wouldn't have left, us knowing how Scarlett's missing put her dad in hospital, I am telling you someone has taken my girls and I want them back."

The room spun she was talking about me! She hadn't moved on she was still fighting for me, I was dead yet, she still held hope and clung to the believe I was alive.

I looked at my dad my big strong larger than life dad, who was a shadow of himself I had done that, me! me missing had done that and now the same man was going to do it again. My dad had been in hospital when I had been missing what was it going to do to him to them, if a year from now they find my sisters cloths and blood? I knew for sure it would kill him, kill them both. I wasn't just saving my sister any more I was saving my whole family.

I watched the lady cop stand

"I'm sorry Mrs Morris I will request Violets missing person case and I will ask the detective in charge to work them both and see if there is a connection".

As my mum stood to see her out she smiled at her, "I will see myself out and keep in touch."

My mum sat back down nodding her head and I knew she was in shock or she would have walked her to the door my mum was one of the people who always saw people to the door, she had made me and Violet do the same for her not to see the police women to the door said a lot about where my mums head was.

I watched as she walked out and then watched as my mum sat with her head down before she took a deep breath and got up.

"Tom go see if your brother is back, I will grab Samsung and take him out for a walk, god knows that dog would live in her room given half the chance".

My dad nodded and walked out I wondered if that meant uncle Jack had moved back he was dad's brother, he had moved away a few years before I went missing but had been talking about coming back.

I hoped he was mum and dad would need him. Samsung was my dog he was a cross between an newfoundland and German Shepard he was pure black and soppy I had rescued him when he was days old and worked with the vet to keep him we had been inseparable but I only realised he was missing when my mum spoke about him, I followed as she walked up stairs to my surprise she walked to where my room was, had been.

I didn't want that door opened I wasn't ready for what was behind the door, I thought about walking away but if Samsung was there then there was where I needed to go.

As my mum opened the door I closed my eyes counting to ten before I opened them I braced myself for the change I would see.

It's hard knowing that my room was probably changed after all this time I didn't expect it to be the same but you still wish it would be slowly I walked to the door and stopped in shock, my room was still my room nothing had been changed it was as if I had never left. Two feelings were running through me and I wasn't sure I like feeling again one was a gladness here was the prove not that I need it that my parents were missing me I know it's wrong to feel glad that they missed me but the fear that I would be forgotten was whatever anyone may tell you a daily thought in your head.

The second feeling was pain what I was putting them through, no it wasn't my thought I had been murdered and that my body hadn't been found but they still had false hope and I was going to destroy that if my body was missing they would still have hope, I was alive somewhere even if that was wrong it gave them hope for my sister but to save my sister I was going to have to destroy that hope and looking around my untouched room I knew it was going to hurt them a lot and no one likes hurting their parents.

I couldn't look at my mum for a minute so I looked to the bed and there was my Samsung sitting on the bed he wasn't moving as my mum called him but the second he saw me he was off the bed and jumping up and down barking in delight my mum looked at him bewildered but he took no notice running around me in circles wagging his tail I smiled

"Hello Samsung. Miss me."
He sat after a few seconds and cracked his head at me as if questioning why I wasn't touching him. My mum had stopped calling him and as I looked up I saw tears running down her face she was sitting on my bed watching him.
"You're here aren't you Scarlett."
She looked down and nodded her head, pressing one hand to her mouth she gasped before talking in a chocked up voice.
"He never reacts like that with anyone but you. If you're here that means you're dead."
She breathed in before looking up at the celling.
"I will still look for you. My baby, I won't stop till your home here with us where you belong. But please look for your sister, I think, I think she needs you."
I watched my mum as she cried in my room and knew she knew I wasn't coming back. walking over to her I touched her check, the tears running down, I know I couldn't touch them but I tried anyway, when I couldn't take it any more I kneed in front of her.
"I will I promise I will bring her back."
Standing back up, I nodded to myself, taking a deep breath. Yes I know I didn't need it but it help me focus I turned and whistled to Samsung to follow and walked out the room down stairs. I could hear my dad talking, walking to the front door I saw it

was open and pointed to Samsung to slip through the door and down the stairs out of the house before dad saw him go.

I saw he was talking to uncle Jake telling him about Violet slowly I walked down the road away from my home Samsung walking next to me, I didn't think where I was going I just knew a plan was forming in my head and the clock was ticking.

As if by magic my body was calling to me not In a voice or anything but deep down inside I felt a small pull and just followed it with Samsung at my heel, I didn't know didn't have a clue what to do from here, but I had the dog now I needed to get the cops.

The sun was starting to disappear when the house finally came into view I had to walk because I couldn't disappear Samsung would be lost, I needed him he stayed by my side the whole time and I remembered how much I missed having him. The sad thing was the house the cop kept us in wasn't that far from where we lived, but I now understood why no one heard us scream it was placed in a small wood land area away from the main stream of people and houses, that was where he was burying our bodies as well I was looking down at Samsung as an idea formed in my head, I wondered if it was a good one I needed to think of my mum and dad now, but I guess in a way it could help them as well for now I needed Samsung to rest it may not be far but walking it, it took a few hours.

I guessed judging by the sun and how far it had dropped in the sky he needed to rest and I needed to check on my sister.

CHAPTER FOUR

I told Samsung to sit by a tree to my shock he did, I walked away from him I didn't want him to see where I was going and I knew he would stay till I came back. I had taught him that as a puppy to stay I would take him to the shops with me sometimes and he had learned to sit and wait for me.

Going round a tree I looked to see if he was still there he was laying down which was a good sign looking towards the house I double checked you couldn't see him, then when I was sure you couldn't I closed my eyes and willed myself to my sister.

She was sitting up and I could hear creaking of the floor as the killer moved around upstairs some of the floor boards creaked, it's funny while I had been with the other women I don't remember hearing those boards creaking, but now with my sister I did, ever thing was clear it was like I had been sleeping but now I was awake you know like after an all-nighter you walk out into day light and ever thing is that little bit sharper and your like wow only this was more, I found each creak sent a shot of fear down me and some part of me was glad I was dead, he couldn't hurt me anymore, he couldn't touch me the fear stayed no matter how much I told myself he couldn't touch me the fear was still there eating away and I couldn't shut it off looking over to my sister I knew the second she realised what the sound was her eyes went wide and her face went white, she looked around and pulled at the chains holding her again, this time the pulls were only half hearted.

I could tell she knew she wasn't getting free her wrists were red raw and she had dried blood on her arms where she had been trying to get free the whole time I had been gone I guessed.

We both looked up as the door opened I turned to her and whispered.

"I'm here."

But she didn't hear me, so I stood by her as we both watched him walk down the stairs with a smile on his face and a hammer in his hands.

I had to do something anything I couldn't let him touch her the pure anger burned the fear away at the thought of him touching her, as I stepped in front of him he walked right through me he started whistling I had forgot the whistling. It stretched my nerves it felt like nails down a chalk board looking over to Violet I could see her curled around herself trying to make herself as small as possible, as if that would make any difference see that's the thing about self-defence is it's all about getting away from the person attacking you they don't tell you how to get out of being tied up with a rope and nowhere teaches you how to deal with being captured by a mad man.

We all go about thinking we are safe and when were not we don't know what to do.

As I stood there watching my sister curled into herself I knew I would make a deal with the devil himself, if I could only save her I watched as he pulled a leg out and knew what he was going to do I thought about getting Samsung but he was just a dog and I couldn't open the door to get him in. He brought his hand with the hammer up I walked to my sister and tried to hold her I closed my eyes as the hummer came down on her right leg the shame running through me at not being able to watch it he had broken something in me and it hadn't been fixed I could no longer watch him hurting and killing, not even as a silent testimony to my little sister. I bowed my head in shame as I heard the crunch and her scream which followed the burning rage inside me raged at the helplessness and I screamed to the heavens I opened my eyes finding the strength from somewhere and watched as my sister screamed in pain as he raised his arms to bring the hammer down again.

"Help me please."

I didn't know who I was asking or even why I had asked for help so many times as I had lay there in pain, but nothing had answered no one had come yet I found myself whispering over and over for someone to help Violet, we both watched and waited for the hammer to full and as the seconds ticked by I realised no one was moving.

Then I heard the sound of the rustling wings once again I looked to the shadows and there he stood. I watched as he walked out of those same shadows over to where we all were my sister and the cop frozen in time he was dressed as he had been last time but this time I got a closer look he was more frightening up close.

"I cannot stopped what is happening I'm not allowed, I'm sorry for your sister little one and the pain she has to go through at his hands, he will be dealt with when it's his time but I can and will do this."

He nodded his head and time renewed its self I looked at him question wondering how he had helped when I heard the phone looking at the cop I watched him drop his hand

"Looks like you may get lucky girl."

My sister didn't look up still sobbing into her arms the pain still to fresh I watched as he walked up to the door and followed pass the reaper to interested on the phone to be scared, I listened as he was called in and breathed a sign of relieve as he cleaned the hammer and put it away.

I watched him take the drug out and walk down to my sister again I turned to follow but the reaper was in my way. He stopped walking so I stopped I didn't even see him move one second he was in front of me, the next he was at my back he stood so close I could feel the burning heat from him he bent his head down and breathed me in I held my breath as he nuzzled my neck.

"You don't have time to nurse your sister if you want to save her. You only have a day left use the time I have given you, know she will be safe for a few hours do something with it."

I gritted my teeth knowing he was right but admitting it to myself and him was hard, all I wanted to do was check she was ok and maybe see if I could talk to her again if the drugs let her but I know I didn't have time.

He breathed me in one last time then he was gone again to stand in front of me.

"You interest me, not a lot does, but I get bored easy don't push it."

I nodded to the Reaper but when I looked up he was gone and the killer cop was changing into his uniform.

I followed him to his car staring a death stare at him the whole way, I had watched Ghost with my sister when I was little and boy was I wishing that it was true! But it wasn't and nothing happened to him as he got into the car.

I blinked myself to where he had driven to it was the police station I followed as him walked in it was different to the one where they were investigation my disappearance. It was smaller, he seemed well liked other police smiled at him as he stopped to get a coffee from their drink machine.

I watched as another cop slapped him on the back and a female cop smiled at him he smiled back at her, I was the only one to see him watch her as she walked away was the only one to see the cold creep into the pretend warmth but seconds later the cold was gone and he was the happy cop, no one knew.

I wanted to scream at them he was a killer and was a liar why couldn't they see that I followed him deeper into the police station and watched him sit down he was laughing and joking with someone sitting across from him. Turning I looked into the room and found a shadow it followed a man who was leaving the station I watched as it looked up and saw me, it frightened me and I wanted to run but before I could it detached its self from the surrounding shadows and I found myself looking at the Reaper, he had changed he looked like he was death, his scythe was in one hand then he winked at me before he raised his hood and followed the man away out of sight. Maybe he was right I didn't want him to be mad at me.

I had a thought so I closed my eyes and returned to Samsung, who was looking into the woods, I tried to think how I could get someone here and hit on an idea looking down at Samsung I frowned and wondered if I could go through with it as I weighed the pros and cons I knew it would work I didn't have anyone else to talk to and I was running out of time.

"Come."

I called to Samsung I had to clear my non existing throat before I could talk and I knew it was all in my mind but my mind agreed with the dry throat so I went with it.

I knew this was going to hurt my mum and dad and I knew it was a terrible idea, but it was the only one I had, and I didn't have time to come up with anything better.

It had taken us longer then I thought to get here we had to keep going back and stopping it was hard not being able to help Samsung, he had been fantastic I wished I could give him a treat he had done exactly what I had asked of him stopping each time and dropping where I asked him to drop. There was one place I wondered if we were going to be able to hide I didn't need anyone spoiling my plan before I had the chance to set it up, but we were fine the journey back was going to take twice as long but I knew that, I was relying on the cops following to see where my trail led.

Now we were at the end or the beginning, it was a start of something or the end of me letting go of my body whichever way you wanted to look at it something was going to happen.

I took a deep breath I hoped that there was going to be councillors where I was going to, I was going to need one after this day was thought looking up at the sky I was glad to see that it was mid-afternoon from the looks of the sun having no idea what the time was hard but we had started early in the morning as soon as the light had hit, so I was hoping that the light would last guessing from the people we hid from on are way to my mum and dads it was summer, people were out early the day light shining and they were in shorts and T shirts so I was guessing we had till late night before it got too dark that should give enough time for them to be led where I needed them to go.

Taking a breath I kneeled down to Samsung I then let him run up to the front door and watched as he barked and scratched to be let in. To my relieve my mum opened the door Samsung ran in passed her his job now finished I knew he would be looking for some food.

I watched as my mum turned to follow him in stepping forward I felt a small pulse of panic she hadn't looked down and she was going to miss it.

A crow cawed and flew at the door missing it by inches before turning and flying off, both me and my mum jumped and watched a black feather flutter to the ground only we watched as it didn't land on the ground but on something else and I watched as my mum frowned, she bent down and started to scream. I looked away, I didn't want to see my mum's face turning I looked over to the trees where the crow had come from and flew back to and found he was there standing watching his wings matched the crows I nodded in thanks knowing that it was him who was responsible for the crow, he acknowledged with a small salute then I blinked and he was gone.

I took a deep breath and followed my mum into the house where all hell was breaking loose.

She had left my gift by the door screaming at my dad to ring the police and to look outside I watched from the side where Samsung sat next to me I watched with a heavy heart which felt as if I was drowning, as mum sat on the table and burst into tears and I had to admit maybe it hadn't been a good idea, as my dad waited outside for the cop who was on my case to come over I watched as my mum sat , she blew her noise and straightened her shoulders, I jumped as she started to talk.

"I know you're here Scarlet, I'm not sure what message your trying to send but I'm guessing you have a plan before you leave here, so I will follow however I can and will leave the fate of Violet in your hands."

I watched as her shoulders slumped and I hear her whisper.

"God help me, if I am wrong and I have just spoken to thin air."

I looked down at Samsung I couldn't hug my mum but he could, pointing to my mum I told him to go and watched as he walked up to her and wined till she put her arms around him I left them in the kitchen while I went to check up on dad, I found him smoking a cigarette.

"Mum will kill you if she finds you smoking."

I told him as I sat next to him but he kept puffing not hearing me so I sat with him a silent support.

It was the one thing I found the hardest thing being dead not being able to help those I loved.

Finally the cops showed up there was about four cars that surprised me to my great relieve the killer cop wasn't with them but the nice one cop who was trying to look for me and my sister as I watched as they walked up to my package Samsung had delivered, as one cop started to take pictures the other cop walked over to my dad, they nodded at each before dad walked him in, calling to my mum that they were here I walked in to see my and dad take a seat at the table.

I stood to the side watching and listening as they talked.

"So Mr and Mrs Morris can you tell me what happened?"

I waited as one of the police officers made tea handing one to my mum and my dad the nice cop, my nice cop refused a cup he looked down at his hands before looking back at both of them.

"It's Scarlet isn't it?"

My mum asked holding on to a cup of tea mum was one for drinking tea all the time, anything wrong let's have tea.

"We don't know that yet Mr Morris."

"Sarah. My name is Sarah."

I looked at my mum she sounded tired as if she had said the same thing to him more than once.

I frowned wondering why he would use her name? The cop, I didn't feel right calling him nice cop if he was going to be horror able to my mum, nodded his head before he continued.

"We don't know that, without doing a DNA testing, right now we are more concerned with were the rest of the body is, how did you come to find the arm?"

Mum sighed

"We didn't."

I watched as she looked to where Samsung laid next to me, he was painting slightly and watching them talk.

"Our daughter's dog brought it back, he went missing last night when he returned he was carrying her arm."

Everyone looked at the dog another cop walked into the kitchen and I watched as the cop decided to call him for the minute he got up and walked into the hall with the other cop following him I followed them both to see what was going on.

"Look everywhere, we need to get someone in here with Cadaver dogs and get a warrant for the garden to be dug up."

The new policeman nodded his head, making notes before he stopped and looked back to the kitchen when he saw no one had followed he asked a question.

"Do you think they killed both their girls?"

I chocked... I hadn't even thought that they would think my parents had done it, this wasn't right!

"Well it would explain why both girls' have gone missing maybe the youngest found something I thought the first daughter was the work of the serial killer we are now tracking which was why I took the case on.

I don't know maybe they are copy cats. One thing is for sure I think the mum is right that arm out there belongs to Scarlett which means the rest is or still is out there somewhere".

"I am waiting for a warrant to search the rest of the house, I don't want to ask them, I don't think they had anything to do with this but it's hard not to think they may have something to do with the murders I want to rule them out straight away, they have been through enough."

"If they are innocent then someone has it in for this family, and now they have just found out that their daughter they hoped was still alive is not only dead but cut up and exposed to the elements somewhere.

We need to get that arm to the forensic team back at the station and get all the information we can from it, it could tell us where she is and in doing so tell us where Violet is, because if she is still alive and it is the serial killer then she doesn't have long that's for sure."

"It's not them, I sure of it."

The cop finished he shook his head and I knew my faith in him was right, he didn't believe my mum and dad had done this but he had to check it out. I needed to think, I didn't have time for this Violet was running out of time and so was I couldn't leave my parents they had been drawn back into the case of me missing, yes they would be proved innocent the second they check they had an alibi of the time I went missing they had been at a family party.

I should have been going to the party that night later on my mum and dad had been at my nan's house all day so I know they were in the clear because of my murder being at that time.

I should have just took my arm to the police station or just dropped it somewhere but even as I thought that, I know they would have still came to the same conclusion because I had used Samsung.

Samsung! Of course I needed to get him to get the cop to follow him. I run through the walls back into the kitchen where Samsung was standing in front of my mum.

"Bark "

I told Samsung so he did,

"Walkies. " I told him and watched as he ran back and forth from the door to the kitchen barking, I watched as they all looked at him.

Mum got up but was stopped by the police officer who had made the tea early on, who then nodded at the young female cop to let him out, no one followed him, I needed another plan it would take too long to find someone to help with the collecting of the body parts and get something else of me.

I needed them to follow but to understand it was Samsung who knew where to go.

Outside my arm had been covered and removed so I couldn't get him to grab it again and the truth be told it made me feel queasy.

Each time I looked at it I was trying to distance myself from the fact that I was using my own body to get them to find us, but each time I was wavering I just thought of my sister and what she was going through.

Samsung was sniffing around in the garden when I noticed a man watching him looking closer I could see a badge on his jeans, so they were watching Samsung after all.

Of course I could have smacked myself they would watch him he as he had found my arm, they would be hoping he would lead them to the rest of my body but they wouldn't want to scare him off!

I stood behind the man who was watching him and blew into his ear, nope nothing, he didn't even flinch disappointed I moved away I know I'm wasting my time no one could see or feel me but I felt the need to test that all the time.

You have no idea how crazy it makes feel, knowing your invisible and having no one to talk to.

Don't get me wrong I know the animals can see me trust me that's what kept me sane but the need to talk to and be seen by other people is a pain which norms away at you.

Whistling at Samsung I walked over to the fence if they wanted the rest of the body then I will get the rest of the body, but to my horror the man stopped Samsung from jumping the fence he held on to his collar while calling for help to get him back inside.

I stood there watching as my only hope disappeared into the house I didn't have time for this he could come back to finish my sister at any time.

Blinking I returned to her and found her sitting up staring into space walking over to her I whispered her name, my heart breaking at the look of hopelessness on her face.

"Violet."

I whispered my eyes widened as she seemed to snap out of her stare and looked around,

"Who's there?"

With hope rising in me I moved closer.

"It's me Violet, Scarlett."

She started to moan and rock back and forth, I took a step back disappointment a stone in my heart but then she spoke again and I knew the drug was the answer.

"Scarlett? You dead? Where are you? Mum and dad miss you."

Taking a breath I answered her

"I'm dead Vil the man who has you killed me, but I won't let him have you Vil I promise."

"No good, Scar no good must be dreaming."

I watched as her head lopped down she was too drugged up, I was talking to my sister and at that minute I didn't care I only cared that she could hear me.

"You hold on Vil, just hold on I will get you out of here."

"Miss you so much Scar."

She whispered back, I blinked myself out of there to my mum and dads again only everyone including mum and dad were gone.

There was a lone policeman standing watching at the front door.

Blinking into the living room I noticed there was police tape in the back garden, turning around slowly I didn't even begin to know where everyone was, all I could guess was that they had took mum and dad away to question them about my arm, check everything out again see if anything would change not that it would and I guess see if they could help them.

 From watching some shows I guessed that they had took Samsung to see what was in his coat and feet least I hoped that was what was going on it made sense. But where were the police who should be searching my house where I didn't know and I hadn't banked on them taking Samsung away.

 I had hoped he was still here that they would check him out here not elsewhere but he wasn't in the house it felt empty and I knew he wasn't there without looking it was something we ghosts felt the emptiness it was like a small hole inside.

I stood in the middle of the living room with the feeling of helplessness knowing time was running out and the plain hadn't worked I didn't know what to do the plan had been simple it should have worked but now instead of helping I had made things worse my parents were now being questioned about my arm who hated them and what was the connection between them and the serial killer but truth be told I wanted to know that one as well I mean who go's after sister's the others had sisters I had seen some at the police station some of the times when I popped in to see how things were going on the times I woke up for a while I knew they would be asked as to where they thought my sister was. The problem was they wouldn't be able to help we had never been to the woods where I laid and we didn't know the killer cop, there was no connection.

  Every second counted and now all eyes would be turned away from looking for her and concentrated on my family home and family trying to find the connection that just wasn't there and I could tell them.

In the mean time I would run out of time to save Violet and she would die a horrible painful death and I had failed them all.

Us ghosts were very good at bring ourselves down that I had noticed but it didn't stop me from the feeling of helplessness and horror.

I needed to make it right but I only now had a night and a day left before I was going to be moved on ready or not.

Suddenly the room got a lot darker and I heard the sound of rustling wings spinning around I saw the grim reaper standing there watching me his wings were folded back and he was leaning against the wall in the living room watching me.

"Well I didn't think you could mess, it up but boy I was wrong. What a right royal mess you have made."

He pushed against the room and walked over to the sofa and sat down spreading his black feathered wings behind him, he was watching me squirm the whole time.

"I don't know what to do."

I whispered in a small voice, he was kind of intimidating me a little, but mostly I was feeling hot. He again had no shirt on and man did he have a body to look at, his lips twisted it was as if he could read my mind and grasped amazed at how human I felt in his presence as if I wasn't a ghost at all, but a young silly girl with a crush on the older man who knew exactly how she felt.

He flicked his fingers to the TV and it came to life, "Watch."

He whispered to me and I looked to see if there was ice in the air his words sounded so cold there was nothing, so I turned to watch the television and found a news reader talking."

"Here at the park today a man found a hand with clothing belonging to what we believe maybe of a victim who went missing two years and may be the first brake in the missing girls' case.

Also this morning a news report came in of the missing girl's family being questioned in connection with the disappearance of Scarlet who had disappeared two years ago. They had believed she had been taken by the missing killer but now it seems that the police could have been wrong as parts of a body with the same clothing was recovered at the family home this morning.

  What's interesting is the younger sister of Scarlett, Violet has also gone missing and hasn't been seen in a month, her car and belongings had been found abandoned and had at first police believed the poor family had lost another daughter to the Missing Killer as his calling card had been found.

"Now questions are being asked if the family are involved with the missing of the two girls.

Of course that was until an hour ago when another part of what the police believe is Scarlet had been found by a man walking his dog in this, a long way from the family home. But what the family has in connection to this and the missing killer remains to be seen.

That all we have for now but we will keep you up dated as the news comes in.

I watched the report before turning to where the reaper was but truth be told I didn't really see him or anything at that moment. My thoughts turned inwards at the news they had found some of me on a foot path like some rubbish, it hurt I looked down rubbing where my heart should be missing the comfort of its beating I had come to turns with being dumped in a forest somewhere, I had accepted that, I had been whole and I knew that when they found me I would be in bits now because I had let Samsung dig me up I felt guilty because digging me up he had dug up the others as well. They were now just laying there for anything which came along exposed to all the elements and creature's.

What if a fox or some other animal came and ripped one of the other girls apart their family would go through what I was putting my family through.

Maybe it was wrong but to me it was worse at least I had the excuse I was doing it to save my sister they were just going to be exposed and left in the open for anything walking by.

I wasn't sure what was right or wrong anymore, it hurt I was surprised how much it hurt I felt foliated and that didn't sit well with me.

I knew I needed to go back to see what they had found what had happened to me. I nodded to the reaper he was looking at me but I couldn't really see his face he had donned his cloak at some point he now looked more like the grim reaper in the pictures, everything felt like a dream even him at that moment, I need to get my head back in the game as I could feel myself fading out like I use to, but this time I held on.

CHAPTER FIVE

I blinked out I opened my eyes and looked down at the grave it brought me rushing back till everything was crystal clear again.

I looked down to where my bones had been I expected to feel horror but nothing came, I wasn't fully back yet but I could feel the horror deep down and welcomed it at that moment I looked down at the space where I had laid for nearly two years and all I felt was satisfaction that I wasn't there anymore.

I had took back control of my body I had done what I wanted to do and began to get the power back, he was living on borrowed time. We, me and the others. We were close to going home and being buried away from here somewhere, where some one cared for us.

I stood there for a second wasting a few precious moments, but ones I found I needed.

I watched the sun light filter and dance in the leaves shining down where me and so many others were buried, it was as if the sun knew about us and wanted to shine for us the way it flittered through the leaves it was like a kiss on our grave and the bodies which lay within.

It gave me a little comfort that thought, that not everything had forgotten us, I nodded once I knew things were changing things had been set in motion and no matter what we would be found.

I just needed to save Violet before she became another body to be uncovered.

The sun seemed to darken for a second and I felt a cold wind something I shouldn't have been able to feel.

He had followed me I didn't think he would but one second I was staring at the bodies alone, the next I felt arms wrap around me something I hadn't felt in like forever something to hold I found myself breaking down he turned me and I wrapped my arms around him I didn't care who he was, his cloak was gone and he was a warm body I could touch who understood me in that second, as I cried I felt his wings surround me, they were so soft and warm.

Everything about him said cold, yet he was hot he didn't say anything and I was grateful for that as I cried for the first time about me. we stood, him holding me and me leaning into him for a while I don't know how long but he made me feel like everything was going to be ok, slowly I felt his wings unwarp from me and I pulled away wiping my tears when I looked up he was staring down at the bodies with a frown on his face before he looked at me again sadly he stepped away.

"I have to go I'm needed."

I nodded I watched as his cloak rolled over him like mist it didn't frighten me this time.

I felt safe something had changed between us. I didn't know what in the last few minutes it had then he was gone, one minute he was there the next gone shaking myself I blinked and I found myself in the middle of chaos, it looked like the beginning of a hunt at my home, well mum and dads.

While I had been away I could see that they had searched the home people were walking in and out some were carrying boxes looking into one I saw things belonging to my sister, a man walked out of the house carrying a machine he was shaking his head and I saw my cop standing there I walked over to him to listen,

"There is nothing around?"

"Small bodies the size of a cat was the biggest we dug it up as the body had been dismembered but that is all we have found. There is nothing there if there had been a body there is no sign or trace of it here, besides the new findings indicates the body was half buried so we are looking for a shallow grave, the soil in the garden doesn't match the one found on the arm and Samsung. She had been exposed for a while before she was moved nothing point to here."

I watched him nod his head in agreement that's all I needed to clear the parents they are down at the station at the moment going over old ground and trying to think of someone who would have a grudge against them, as they were targeted twice none of the others missing with sisters have had anyone else going missing in their families."

I breathed a sign of relieve mum and dad were in the clear again that was when I noticed that uncle was there looking after Samsung he had him on the lead and was talking to another man who had a police coat on but was plain clothed.

 I watched as he handed Samsung over to him with a nod and then walk back into the house smiling I walked over to where Samsung could see me I knew what they were going to try and do and I was all for it, this was what I had worked for, so I decided let's start.

 I signed for Samsung to begin,

" Find me."

 I called to him knowing we had played this game all the time I would take him to somewhere and show him, something then send him to find it only this time he knew where to look and what to find it didn't matter that it was bits of me it was just a game to him.

 I was standing there so he didn't think anything of holding something of me it smelled of me and I was there smiling and praising him so in his mind it was a game. He pulled the policeman barking and wining the policeman who was holding him held him back from running he called over to my cop and I hear his name for the first time.

"Chisco?"

I watched my cop look up, I watched as he took in the way Samsung was fighting the lead and then he looked to where a car was parked at the nod of another man standing by a car he called back to the policeman holding Samsung .

"Let him go they will follow his lead for a while see if it works I will be along in a minute just need to finish up here and sign off."

With that we were off I noticed two police dogs jump out the car and follow Samsung behind keeping far enough away not to distract him but also working at looking for signs of my body we ran to the park close to home where he sniffed out the first part it was just a finger I had been running out before we got home and had started leaving small things I also didn't need anyone finding bits of me god if a child had found me I would never be able to forgive myself.

 We hit the local park where I had left the last or first of my finds and Samsung did me proud he shot straight to it the policeman holding him stopped him short of picking it up lifting his arm he cried halt and every one stopped.

So here we stood in the park where they found something belonging to me I watched as it was cornered off more cars turned up and the place was shut down.

I could see police looking for more parts they had a few dogs wondering back and forth each handler had a bag with some of what I was guessing were my clothes in but they weren't following the trail, Samsung was pulling trying to get them to follow him but he was being held back.

They seem to want to comb the area but they wouldn't find anything there was nothing there to find it was on the trail a bit away from here.

"The crows."

I hadn't heard him behind me and jumped a mile high when he spoke the cold from his words hit me making me shiver I hadn't felt the chill which always announced his arrival and the fear I normal felt was missing as I turned I saw the ripper smiling at me and I knew he found it funny how he could make me jump.

"Don't you have somewhere to be? And what do you mean the crows?"

He turned to ice at my first question but relaxed a small bit at my second question, his wings raised a bit as he nodded to the birds in the trees, they are how you ended up here carrion birds."

I nodded in understanding.

"As to why I'm here you interest me and I was bored."
I decided to jump on that,
"Do you have many friends? What do you do besides collect ghosts?
I watched as he laughed and found he looked younger he was fascinating to watch but scary as well like a tiger at the zoo, only he wasn't in a cage safely away from me and he wasn't a tiger, but a male who was standing near me and who could end my ghost existence before I could help my sister. Yet I couldn't look away couldn't stop the fascination of him.
"Do you have a name?"
He smiled at me but it was a sad smile
"No." he replied
"I am what I am I have no name no history I live to take and do my job."
I felt so sad for him and when I was gone he would have no one for no one would talk to the ghost who took them the reaper who was in the black cloak hidden from view and breathed ice no matter how beautiful he was they would never see never know. Rubbing my arms I watched him watch the dogs
"I will call you Rip."
I told him I felt better and he didn't reject it he nodded his head once in acknowledgement and I felt a small secret pleasure from him I smiled to myself everyone should have a name.

"Where do I go from here?"
I asked turning from him and watched as the police searched the grass land around I knew they weren't going to find anything the rest of me I was still were I had been left the birds hadn't took much.
I felt he walk up close to me,
"You know I cannot help you I'm not allowed, your time is running out why does it have to be your dog who helps you there are others?"
I watched the other dogs as they worked thinking it thought before I dismissed it
"Those other dogs don't know me it's quite a walk from here and they are on leads I don't think that that would work."
"Well looks like your luck may be changing."
I turned to him wondering what he meant but found only air he had gone, but it was ok I saw what he had meant the second I turned, the cop Cysico who had been at my mum and dads had just pulled up.
I was sure that wasn't right but I wasn't questioning my good luck moving over to the car I signed for Samsung he started to bark getting the cops attention but he just walked over to another cop, frustration bit at me I hated needed others to do thing but not be able to tell them what they needed to do.

I wish I knew the time and I knew I needed to get back to my sister I tried to bite one of my nails but of course there were no nails to bite.

I screamed in frustration and saw Samsung tilt his head to look at me I smiled at him and he lay down for a minute before jumping up again and pulled the man holding him in the right direction this time Cysico turned he frowned at Samsung before nodding to the cop

"let him go, give him his lead he wants to go somewhere and so far his led us to her each time, a team will follow to bag anything you find we will set up a team depending on what we find one person stays with the find the others move off."

CHAPTER SIX

They followed Samsung as he ran pulling at the end of the lead pulling them out of the park into a country type path, it was more of a dirt track with trees on both sides hidden in a small hole in one of the trees there was another finger again they called a halt, this time the finger was bagged and tagged and I listened as my cop spoke.

"We need to get others out here I'm starting to think we are going to find a lot more, let him lead, see where he takes us we will tag anything we find and others can come behind us and collect the evidence.

If I'm right we need to move fast before anything is picked up by wildlife or reporters and before we lose light."

One of the other cops with him nodded

"Why do you thing this has suddenly happened?"

I listened with interest to his answer.

"The dog has found her I'm guessing. He must have been trying to bring her home where ever she was. Or the killer is playing a sick game with us and using the dog for some sick reason, whatever the reason is, he is giving us a lead we haven't had in two years, maybe if we found her we find the other missing girl's so let's give him the lead and let him take us to her when we get to the site maybe we will finally know what had happened to her."

"So your still convinced it's a serial killer?"
I watched as Cyscio nodded his head. We moved on till we hit a small road we needed to cross to get to the open field beyond.

I saw another police car pulling up I didn't take much notice till I saw who was driving and was now getting out of the car.

If I was still alive I know I would have thrown up there and then, it was my killer! he was walking up to the cop's and shock hands before they smiled at each other and carried on walking I couldn't breathe I repeatedly told myself I'm dead, I'm a ghost I don't need to breath! Hell I was talking to myself I needed oxygen to talk, not that I needed oxygen I was dead. Over and over I repeated it but I could still feel myself being pulled down into memories.

I was back in that hole I could smell the rotting flesh around me of other girls gone before and hear the sound of his treads as he walked across the room.

I couldn't move my head it felt to heavy and I was so tired I lay there on the cold firth floor shivering so frightened I couldn't draw breath he started to talk

"Ah my sweet, sweet Scarlet, your blood is as red as your name."

From the corner of my eye I could see the flash of a knife,

"I will show it to the world and bath in it by the time I am done with you."

I could hear his whispers in my ear as he bend down next to my head. I remember thinking why is he whispering? When no one can hear. I lay there helpless, the drugs soaking into my body refusing to let me move holding me hostage to his will.

The words sank in then the defeat crawled over me there was no escape. I closed my eyes as the knife got closer I felt cold then something heavy landed in my hand my eyes snapped open and I was at the road again.

I looked to my hands and found a feather in them I knew straight away it was one of Rips, I didn't need to see the colour to tell just the feel of it solid in my hands told me everything I needed to know.

I closed my eyes in thanks he had pulled me back showed me away to escape from that time and place. Finally my head listened and I sorted myself out least I knew even been ghost I could still get a shock.

I felt the small whisper of cold before his words hit me.

"Had I known about you then I would have come I would have stopped him and defied the law, I would have spared you the pain."

As I turned he was nowhere to be seem he was gone leaving me with the warmth of his words to me.

I watched as the killer walked over to where Cysco was talking to another police man they had stopped because I had stopped Samsung, when I saw the killer as the cop let Samsung sniff around walking closer but not close enough to distract Samsung.

I listened to what they were saying and found my killer was quietly but expertly questioned Cyscio to see what he knew.

I was guessing that if he was involved my killer wouldn't need to be doing that as they would both know what the other knew and there would be a small amount of panicking at least, well I would like to think so anyway. I relaxed a little bit as I thought about what to do.

My killer was here, that meant my sister was safe for the time being, it also meant I couldn't let Samsung show the cop where my body was because the killer was here.

I watched him as he walked around as if he owned the park and knew if I could I would kill him right now, anger clouded my mind for a few seconds and I watched as he walked to where they had found a small piece of me. I saw the small frown on his face as he bent down before he straightened and looked towards where Samsung was standing watching me he followed Samsung's gaze I froze for a minute but of course he saw nothing.

I remembered the feeling of sick as I watched him and remembered how I had been sick while he had me, he had stood there and laughed as I lost what little water he had allowed me to have, he hadn't cleaned me up or the place where I had thrown up. It wasn't there now so he must have cleaned it once I was gone I had noticed that about him he cleaned the mess away but left the bloody bits of body there I was sure it was a fear thing.

I realised as I watched him kick at some of the grass as one of the dogs. A Godiva dogs sniffed him showing a lot of interest before the dog handler holding it laughed at something he said and pulled the dog away the dog noticed me for the first time and pulled its handler towards me.

I smiled down at it then moved away I stood quietly and studied my killer out in the day light, thought I had made it a habit of keeping tabs on him when I zoned back in I still hadn't really looked at him, he was tall and good looking and wore his uniform well.

I knew why he had managed to get us women he seemed completely confident in himself and looked like a safe haven one of those cops who would look after you.

He was looking down again when a crow cried he looked up and I saw his frown as he looked to the trees where a few more crows had gathered.

Cyscio walked Samsung over to him I hadn't see him take Samsung from the police handler and I wondered why he did it.

I watched Cyscio watch the killer cop as they talked he kept looking towards the trees where my body and the others were then back to the crows.

I knew he was going to move the girls bodies the second he got a chance I could see in his face he had realised where we seemed to be heading I knew Cyscio hadn't confirmed it was me they were looking for, I was guessing by the way Cyscio was looking at the killer cop he would make sure that no one told him who it was they had found, my suspicions were confirmed a few seconds later as Cyscio called to one of the police officers standing next to the cars I listened as he whispered to him.

"Find out who that cop is and spread it to the rest of the team, I don't want him knowing anything about this, who it is we are looking for and what the investigation is about, this investigation is on lock down."

The other policeman looked to where my killer was talking to one of the dog handlers I watched as the handler looked up towards where we were standing and Cysico responded with a quick shake of his head before he looked away ,so he missed the look my killer throw his way but I was sure he hadn't see the shake of his head so I was guessing he wasn't getting the information he had wanted.

My attention was pulled back to the conversation.

"You think he needs to be looked in to? He,s a cop sir."

"Yes I know, it would make sense wouldn't it how the bodies go missing and there is nothing to show for it. I'm not saying he is but just check him out quietly and say nothing to no one about the killer being a cop.

I don't need anyone being spoken to, if it turns out to be true there is still a girl alive out there somewhere. If we are lucky Violet may still be alive."

The other cop turned and headed for the car so he missed Cysico muttering under his breath.

"But I doubt it."

I Need to move now it was great that Cyscio was on the right track and maybe if I left him he would follow the right trail to the right killer but by then my sister would be dead and that was not an option.

Not just because I was running out of time but now it was a race to get to the dump site before my killer did.

What I had done to myself and family would be for nothing and my sister he was going to be cutting her time short, just so that he could get rid of any evidence laying around on the off chance that they found him, the crows and body parts had spooked him and he was going to cut and run I could see it in his face and the way he kept looking to his car and back to the crows and the strained force smile he gave Cyscio as he passed him.

For the first time I smiled, and enjoyed the panic on his face.

As he walked passed me I heard his radio crackle and he answered it smiling a strained smile at the rest of the police he passed on the way to his car.

I watched him stop for a minute he seem to bend down but straightened straight away and walked quickly to his car, I watched the car turn and drive off. Cyscio turned and back towards his car I blinked to Samsung to follow with a bark which had the other two dogs looking up, he took off towards me as he run pulling the handler with him.

I ran towards the tree but to my dismay the other two dogs didn't follow and after a few minutes of following Samsung stopped and started to pull the other way.

I stopped and watched wondering what the hell I could do, Samsung and the other dogs were pulling the wrong way I tried again and again to get him to come to me but he was pulling in the other direction, I couldn't get them to follow I would have to stand there and watch them go the wrong way the other two dogs had gone back to sniffing for more evidence.

I could see the two other cops looking at each other and shaking their heads they weren't finding anything new and they wouldn't I wasn't there.

I walked over to where Samsung was pulling the handler wondering what had got his attention so bad he took us closer and closer to where the killer had been standing for a few seconds moving in front of Samsung I walked forwards and found what was attracting him, there was fresh meat on the ground dog food by the looks of it.

 I was sure it hadn't been there a little while ago I looked down at it then up to Samsung pulling towards it and I just knew it was put there by my killer I wondered for what reason and then realised he knew who they were looking for.

 Someone had told him and he needed my dog out of the way Samsung would eat it and that would be the end of him dead or asleep he would stop leading them to the dump site giving him time to move the bodies that was why he had come here.
"If he eats that meat, that's the end."
I whispered it out load it didn't stop the horror and fear running through me.
"Stop"
 I told Samsung but he didn't stop and I knew there was something in the meat I wished I could smell it or touch it but I doubted that that would help anyway as I wouldn't know what to look for.

 Anyway I just knew if Samsung touched it, it was game over for him and me and my sister I had no time to come up with another plan and I was now sure that he knew that someone was on to him.
Rip appeared before I could ask him anything he stood in front of the food and bent down till he was

the same height as Samsung then he hissed at him, his eyes flashed and his fangs looked huge as he let out a deep growl.

Mist black as the night poured around him with lighting flashing inside he looked savage and wild, I couldn't take my eyes off him he was so wow, sad I know but that was the only thought my brain could come up with was wow. Samsung had a completely different reaction he stopped and his ears went back his tail slipped between his legs and he turned and ran the other way.

Rip straightened, the mist disappeared with the lightning and his eyes calmed to the mirror sliver I had seen the first time I had seen him, that mist I realised was what stopped me from seeing him in the shadows it hid him from view till he wanted to be seen.

"Go "

He whispered before he disappeared again, I didn't think twice I blinked in front of Samsung and this time he listened and we were off moving fast on the right trail the other handlers pulled their dogs and soon they were running as well, running to keep up with me as I lead them in the right direction.

 I looked through the trees the sun was beginning its slow climb from the sky, so I was guessing it was after three in the morning at least. The dogs didn't look tired but the men running with them did and I knew if the dogs didn't find something soon they would probably call the chase off.

I had got lost the trees all looked the same and I knew that I had left some of my body around here somewhere, but I didn't know where I just hoped we weren't moving to far from the drop zone of my body parts but I wasn't sure of what the protocol was.

Would they keep going I didn't know what I did know was the forest where the bodies were just ahead so I kept moving but the dogs had stopped and seemed to be looking at something on the ground as I watched one of the policemen who had been following raised his hand and the dogs sat even, Samsung seemed to be listening to them as he sat as well, I could see his tongue hanging out, it was then I noticed the crows in the trees again and got a sinking feeling I moved closer to look at what it was that had stopped the dogs and wished I hadn't, on the ground was an eye, trust me when I say I hadn't left the eye both of my eyes had still been in my head when I left the head.

I felt sick rising in my stomach and I knew if I had a stomach I would have been sick there, the worse thing was it wasn't my eye.

Samsung stopped and sat down as the other dogs were the centre of attention this time he hadn't looked for the eye because it shouldn't have been there.

I knew they would use that find as a reason to take a break so I knew I had time to find out where I was and get them on the right path. First I needed to see why bits of bodies had started to appear as a few feet from the eye a handler had called out and there was something else I couldn't make out what it was from where I stood but there was no way I was getting closer to finding out either, it was red and wet that was all I needed to know to stay away I had seen enough to last me more than my life time and then some.

Blinking out to the body dump site I found that the crows were now picking at the uncovered bodies there were marks on the ground showing other animals had been there all the bodies were being pulled and the dirt kicked and pushed away.

I stood there whispering sorry, I moved closer to the other dead girls even knowing they weren't there and didn't care what was happening to their bodies I still felt bad, as I moved closer the crows gave flight and a whole mass of them took off in the flapping of wings till the sky was full of them.

Their cries filled the air and I had never seen so many and I knew this wasn't normal, I was sure Rip had something to do with it but I could use the birds so I blinked back to Samsung he was sitting up looking in the direction of the birds cry and I knew the job was nearly done.

The police were close enough to have seem the birds I could see them frowning at the cry's and looking as suddenly the birds could be seen flying up.

 I knew where I had gone wrong now and using the birds for my direction I called to Samsung and we turned left away from where we had been heading and back to where we had lay the trail.

The handler wanted Samsung to go the other way away from where the other body parts were laying, but I called him and used commands to make him pull for the other way and after a few seconds, the handler gave him his lead and we were off running through the trees and bushes ten minutes later we came to a peace of me, a leg I breathed a sigh of relieve as they stopped tagged and bagged but moved on as Samsung pulled soon we were in the forest where the bodies dump was.

 I watched as the three dog handlers stopped suddenly two of them raised their hands to cover their noses while the third holding Samsung go on to his radio and asked for the cars to be dispatched to pick the dogs up they didn't need them anymore. I waited for a while and soon the forest was swarming with police looking, Cyscio turned up and the three handlers took the two dogs and Samsung away I wanted to follow but I needed to see them find us a young policeman did he called then turned to some trees and lost his stomach contents.

CHAPTER SEVEN

I needed to get back to my sister with one last look I disappeared and reappeared at the killer's house.
I stood for a few minutes just looking at her in the dim light she didn't look good.
Her legs were the wrong way and I knew they were broken at some point he must have come back while I wasn't here, because there was a small bowl of water just out of her reach on the floor.
It looked clean and inviting for someone who hasn't had a drink for who knows how long, he did it to torment her.
I knew it was one of his favourite games he would play with all of us he, would place water and mouth-watering food which smelled so nice so close to us but if you reached for it you it was always placed out of our reach even those girls who could move wouldn't be able to reach it they would end up hurting themselves and in to much pain trying to pull themselves along, he would come in and laugh before turning and walking back out but leave the food there to rot in front of you.
He hadn't put food out this time just water.
She had bruises which hadn't been there before and one of the cuts on her wrist looked infected it was a black colour with yellow running through it.
As I looked closer I could see she was sweating her clothes what was left of them were damp and I was

beginning to wonder if we may have run out of time without him doing anything else to her.

She was still sleeping in the drugs grip, there was nothing more I could do at the moment so my thoughts turned to my mum and dad.

Blinking I thought of them and found myself at police station they were both in different rooms, mum looked grey and I wished I could hold her and tell her everything was going to be ok, I walked up to her and put my hand on her shoulder and felt my heart sink as it went straight through her looking at my hand I felt myself getting angry at it how stupid I felt... but there it was, I was mad at my body because it wouldn't do what I wanted it to do.

I couldn't hold or touch my mum she didn't know I was here, couldn't feel me and understand I was fighting for them the best way, I knew how in this strange place I found myself a ghost alone.

Well no scrap that I wasn't alone, I had the grim reaper with me but he couldn't help me, couldn't touch my mum and even if he could I would have fought him, if he tried to touch any of them at the moment the last thing I needed was them passing over and having the grim reaper touching you was, I was guessing not a good thing.

I moved away from my mum with that feeling which seemed to sit on my shoulders and lay in my heart since this all began that hopelessness and fear. As I stood silently watching her I couldn't leave

her on her own, something in me wouldn't let me
let her sit alone, even knowing time was running
out so fast now but I needed to be with my mum
she had always made me feel safe that everything
was going to be alright and even if she didn't know
it I would be here for her at this moment.
Worry and fear circled my mind about my sister,
but there was nothing I could do.
The bodies have been found and she was asleep so
I couldn't get through to her so I took the little time
out and as the two police officers walked into the
room where my mum sat I watched with pride, she
straightened and looked them in the face, they sat
down and proceeded to tell her about the bodies.
I watched for a few more minutes but I could see
the fight coming back to her as they told her Violet
wasn't one of them, nodding once I decided I could
leave, her colour had come back though the shock
of hearing what was happening left her a little pale.
I knew now all she needed was my dad so I turned
and I walked through the wall where my dad was
sitting in the next room and felt tears gathering, he
was sitting with his shoulders slumped and head
down with one hand on his heart.
Fear ran though me then what if my dad died? He
had a bad heart and what if this made it worse?
The air seemed to stand still in the room for a few
seconds as I felt Rip arrive this time the touch of a
wind against me sent a small shock through me and

I looked at him in surprise, but couldn't tell if he felt it to, he was watching my dad this time he had a shirt on and I couldn't tell if I was disappointed or not the feel of him so close was making me hot and I had to stop to think do ghosts get hot?

I mean you would think they wouldn't as we have no blood but I was feeling hot and I would have sworn that I could feel the blood rushing around.

I turned back to my dad I didn't have time to get distracted but then he spoke

"It's ok he won't die. His not on my list."

I nodded feeling the relieve running through me but I felt myself looking towards the room with my mum.

I watched from the corner of my eye as he looked to where I was looking before I caught a small half smile on his face,

"Or her, They will be fine it's your sister not them you need to be worrying about."

I knew that.

I nodded at him but I couldn't leave my parents, I just needed to know they were going to be ok.

The door opened to my dad's room and I saw my mum standing next to a women, a man walked in and started to talk.

"We have called your brother Jake He is going to come down and get you. Samsung has been taken to our kennels to be fed and cleaned up before we give him back to you. I hope that is ok? "

At my dad's nod he carried on talking
"We just wanted to thank you for your help today."
I watched as he turned and then walked out and I
knew the policeman felt awkward, relieve caused
through me as my dad stood up I watched as he
walked out to my mum and put his arms around
her, they were being spoken to by someone.
 I watched as they nodded with what was said and I
knew they were talking about me and what would
happen now.
 I felt nothing about my body now that I had been
found I felt the weight of it lift from my shoulders
and somehow knew that I was letting go of
something which had kept me here.
 A little more the problems which had kept me here
were slowly being resolved.
But now I needed to face the biggest one of them
all.
Nodding once to Rip who had been by my side the
whole time then I blinked to my sister who was just
waking up.
Walking over to her I wiped my ghost tears away
she had lost a lot of weight he was back I knew that
as he had turned the light on and I could see my
sister clearly for the first time, it was worse than I
had first thought she had marks on her arms and
face which really hurt to look at.
 I knew they were superficial compared to what was
happening to her hands and arm with the black on

it and her legs which were I could see were turned the wrong way her knees were bent at an angle, they shouldn't be looking to the door.

I knew she wasn't going to survive the night if I didn't get her help. The body dump was close to here, I didn't know how close, each time I tried to it work out I couldn't, something went wrong I couldn't walk to the body dump from here and I couldn't walk back from the body dump to here something stopped me. I was hoping that they would come searching, but I wasn't going to hold my breath he would be down the list after what they found today, Cyscio may suspect him but he would be swamped working on what he had.

The feeling Cyscio had wasn't going to be enough with him being a police man. My sister blinked and looked straight at me, but she was clean of the drugs so I knew she couldn't see me.

I stood there wondering what to do for what felt like the thousand time I knew that no matter what was going to happen to me I would never forget this place it haunted me I heard him walk to the door, his foot tread heavy and I now knew from watching him it was deliberate he didn't walk like that he was soft treaded at the station or whenever I saw him walking elsewhere, but here he tread loudly as he walked it was to up the fear letting us know that he was coming it was another mind game he liked to play.

Standing by my sister I saw the fear and hate on her face, I knew she like me knew this time he was coming for her and that she was going to hurt.
We both watched as he walked down to where she laid, he smiled and I saw her sink away into herself I pinched myself as I felt myself fade away.
I knew I couldn't do what I had done for the other, cut and run she was my sister and even if she couldn't see me I had promised I would be here for her.
So I stood and stayed where I was, wishing I was still alive just for a few minutes that's all it would take me to hurt him to stop him hurting my sister.
I watched as he grabbed a foot and just snapped, it the sound of her bone breaking made me black out for a second I couldn't stop myself from trying to hit him, it didn't work I shot straight through him doing nothing to him as he laughed and it didn't make me feel any better.
I watched as my sister threw up from the pain, I knew from experience he wasn't going to stop and he didn't, he didn't let up from hurting her he pulled her hair and hit her again and again all I could do was stand there and wish him dead .As I watched in silent testament to my sisters pain, sobbing I screamed for Rip he was there in an instant freezing time he pulled me into his arms holding me as I screamed and rocked I could feel

the cold leaving him freezing the room but as he held me all I could feel was the warmth from him "This, it's the part I hate of my job."
He whispered as he pulled me away slightly to look at me.
"You have changed me! I didn't see didn't care till you."
"Why?"
I whispered
"Why should I."
He replied
I looked up at him not in horror, I couldn't understand but then he spoke
"They were going to a better place away from what they had gone through what did what come before matter? But watching you and your sister being with you it does matter. But I couldn't do anything any way I'm not a loud to, no interfering, no getting involved, I do my job and that is it."
"And now ?"
I asked but he shook his head,
"I cannot change it, but I understand. I'm sorry Scarlett I know you want me to stop him, to do something but I can't it is forbidden, she will not hurt soon and she will be in a better place."
I felt the pain of betray slice through me as he spoke I don't know why I had expected him to do something but he was right I had.

I felt him withdrew slightly his attention moving from me I could feel the emotions he brought out at his touch fading as he pulled away.

" I have to go."

He bent his head and I felt a kiss of ice on my head before he gathered up his ice and disappeared I was left.

 As time returned to watch as the blows rained down on my sister. I decided I would I wait for her at least we could go together.

 I had failed myself, my sister, my mum and dad. My head hurt I felt heavy and broken.

Standing there I knew it was going to be soon everything I had tried to do nothing had worked and there was no time left closing my eyes I couldn't watch anymore I heard a dog bark just once I opened my eyes and frowned the killer didn't notice and my sister was screaming and in too much pain to notice, But I did, I listened and heard another bark but there were no dogs here and Samsung was back at the police station.

 I walked through the walls to the outside promising my sister I would return in a second.

I walking around the house I couldn't see anything, but I heard barking again, so I looked across to the woods across from the house and found I was right there was a dog barking but it was a dog who shouldn't have been there it was Samsung.

He was standing in the middle of the field between the woods and the house, I could already hear the barking of the other dogs in the distance coming this way but I couldn't understand how he had got there.

I looked for a car or something but there was no one around, Samsung was on his own and upon seeing me he ran across as I turned in a circle I saw a single feather falling from the sky, but no bird insight then I felt the kiss of ice for a second before it was gone thanking him silently knowing he had helped the betray gone I knew what I had to do as Samsung ran up to me I ran back to the house shouting.

"Find Violet find her"

he run to the house I pursed and held my breath for a second as I thought about what I was about to do knowing I could be ending my dogs life but not doing anything would be the end of my sisters life my heart broke I knew it wasn't a choice, he would do what needed doing I stood for a second knowing what that second could cost my sister before I bent down and did the one thing I never thought I would do when I had been told to teach him I turned him from a pet to a guard dog. Samsung sat for a second as I bent down then looking him in the eyes I whispered the command which changed my family dog.

"Samsung protect from the bad person."

I pointed to the door as a scream of pain filled the air and I watched as my dog responded to the pain in that scream and the command in my voice.

He stopped barking and went deadly quite as he looked around then as another scream reached us he bolted into action hitting the door with force he went straight through the window and ran straight for the sounds now coming out of the house where the window was broken.

I didn't go back in I knew the door to the room was open he liked it that way just to show you how helpless you were, like saying here's the door open but no you can't go through it. Instead I went back to the field where the first police offices and their dogs appeared this time the dogs ran to where I was the screams from the house clear and loud in the field the police could hear it and were running to help.

I blinked into the room and shouted stop to Samsung as he was about to kill my killer, he stood over him in front of Violet, his hair was up and he looked twice the size he was, every move my killer made set Samsung off on another round of growling and snarling.

He kept checking up on Violet whipping his head round he whined at her and nudged her before turning and growling at the killer again.

I watched as the police officers ran into the room only to stop in shock at what greeted them there was enough in that room to send him to jail for ever.

He looked up at the police men he knew it as well his face went blank the handler who had worked with Samsung slowly walked to him whispering good boy to Samsung letting him see his hands, but I could tell Samsung wasn't listening he was in protection mode he moved away from the handler back towards Violet but with nowhere to turn he was standing on her legs, she whimpered and Samsung turned to her.

"Good boy Samsung, lay down now, well done good job."

I heard her whisper to Samsung he responded instantly and lay down, the handler approached but Samsung, let him still rumbling a little as the handler got hold of Samsung two police men rushed past to see to Violet, while the other two turned their attention to the killer policeman, then everything happened at once, Samsung suddenly lunged the handler swung round to see what he was going for and the two policemen shouted "No"

As my killer turned and shot himself in the head I closed my eyes at the sight of him.

But I opened them as the ice wind of my Reaper appeared he was in full cloak, his ice mist swelling around and there I saw the grim reaper in all his glory the skull face with the burning eyes black mist like shadows swelled around him snapping at the body, the scythe strong and sharp gleaming in the light, while ice filled the air making it freezing this was someone with no mercy I saw my killers ghost as it tried to run caught by the mist he screamed as it touched him but it swallowed him up in an instant and Rip and the killer were gone in a blink.

Violet cringed as people touched her and cried screaming to stay way she screamed for Samsung the only thing she knew was safe at that minute till the handler with Samsung walked forwards he let Samsung touch her and she draped herself over him crying, he was covered in blood very quickly.

 I could see my sister bleeding over him as someone rushed to her and put a blanket round her.

 Samsung growled at them and I knew he was feeding off Violets fear I knew I need to do something or Samsung was going to lose it there was too much going on to many emotions for him to handle and Violet was a mess he had the need to protect her but there was nothing to protect her from, the bad guy was gone.

I walked over to him smiling I reached down and stroked his head enough Sam good boy enough, he quietened down straight away letting Violet hold him as she was treated.

I stood in the clear fresh light hospital room miles away from the horror, I know it sounds weird calling a hospital room light fresh and airy, but that was how it felt to me after that place the dark damp gut churning hole. I watched as Violet slept for the first time in peace and safety the wires to the machine a gentle reminder in the back ground she was attached to drips one with food and liquid the other her pain meds.

They were attached to her hand feeding into her.

The cut which was so bad had been cleaned and bandaged I hoped they got the infection on time. On each side of her bed were our mum and dad each holding her hand they looked tired but there was a peace to them now.

I knew that they were going to be ok.

As for Violet I didn't know if she would be mentally ok, but I had done all I could my time here was done.

Watching a little longer I felt a whisper of cold wrap its self around me and then it was gone, but I knew he wouldn't come in here it was just a gentle reminder I nodded in acknowledgement knowing he would see and looking one last time I whispered good bye and turned and left.

I blinked and found myself in my home.

I walked around taking it in one last time it was quite, now except for the television playing quietly in the living room my uncle Jack was there sitting watching , he was looking after Samsung till mum and dad could feel safe enough to leave Violet.

Samsung was being treated like a prince he had been returned to mum and dad a few days after the rescue and discovery.

No one knew how he had got there in time or how he had got free, the people at the kennels who had been looking after him swore blind that he had been in the kennel locked in five minutes before he turned up at the grave barking and setting the dogs off running with him.

That was how the police had be so close they were following him and he had lead them there the cctv at the kennels had shown he had just disappeared all it showed was a black feather floating down to the floor.

He had been given back to mum and dad after he had shown he wasn't a threat they had him tested but without the command's I gave him he was just the soft gentle puppy dog and each officer who had been there that day stood up and testified for him he was well liked by the police department.

So now he was home resting, but I stayed away from him it hurt to much to say goodbye it was one to many so I turned and left.

EPILOGUE

I found myself outside, it was a different time, I had moved through time again but I could tell not too far in time.

 I looked at the forest ground some of the soil was still disturbed but most had been put back the holes filled in there was nothing on the ground to look at just new soil.

The forest was quiet and whole once again the scar of the graves wiped away by nature and time.

 I nodded my head to the lone crow sitting on one of the low hanging branches and finally I let go of the chains I hadn't known I had been holding chains from the other girls the feeling of responsibility and guilt which had been wrapped around, they had been put to rest every girl had been found and returned home to their family.

 I needed no longer to stand guard as a silent witness, guard to us all, others now knew our story.

 My sister may be a little bruised and battered for now but she was strong and she would be, she didn't need me any longer and my mum and dad could let me go and start the grieving.

 My time now was my own, I was no longer needed here it was time for me to go I looked up to where the Rip stood I had heard him arrive but had been drawn back to the beginning and now I needed to say good bye.

I looked around one last time before nodding to him answering his unspoken question, I knew why he had helped me, why he had followed me the feeling was mutual, he nodded back and I felt a great weight on my back, looking over my shoulders I found white wings beautifully matching his black ones.

Lifting them I found the knowledge and strength flood my body and mind so with a though I turned and followed him thought the trees and into the sky leaving my old life behind.

He held out his hand and I closed my around his answering his silent question, he smiled and I folded my wings letting him hold me close and fly me to where ever we were going I would stay with him and help him, even death needed a friend a lover someone to care for and be cared by and I would be his.

RIP'S FIRST VIEW OF SCARLET

Rip had seen the house on his list, knew there was a ghost there who needed to move on so he had decided to check her out.

He watched day after day, night after night he found himself drawn back to her to the same place just to watch her as she drifted in and out of time and view lost between here and now so he couldn't help once he had reached for a touch to let his figures touch her hair but even his figures passed through her as if she wasn't there he wondered if he somehow imagined her, dreamed her up one cold lonely night, but he didn't have the imagination to dream of someone so beautiful so bright her spirit hurt his eyes. He had seen her when he had came for another watched as she sat helpless and alone locked in her grief. Till one night he had been fighting a demon and losing when he had felt the shift which had told him another spirit was ready to leave but something had felt different, he had killed the demon the need to go giving him the strength and power he had needed and blinked to the spot of the spirit to find himself looking at her. She was whole and real, a ghost he could finally touch her and feel her, he had to move her on but he didn't want to, the thought of not seeing her again, for the first time made him wonder what would happen if he just let her be.

As he watched her he saw her in so much pain, for the human she was looking at and he knew he needed to do something.

Slowly he let himself form, slowly relieving himself to her and his breath caught as she turned to look at him, he knew he would do anything and everything in his power to make her his.

Preview of

Kiss of fire

PREFACE

You may think I am just a helpless young woman, lost and alone, but you would be wrong, I am your mistake, your nightmare, the silent storm you let into your home. You were wrong, you slipped, now watch your mistake, and I will be what I must to survive, to get strong, to bring my fire.

I will never be your victim.

Before my story is finished there will be the heat of the fire and blood spilt into the night. Love found and revenge satisfied, no one takes that which is mine and thinks they can hold it for long.

I will get my brother back and nothing and no-one will stop me, not even the frosty kiss of a cold night. I will bring the wind, and fire will return and the world and you will burn in the heat and fire with me and we that you thought you could strip and control us will survive.

CHAPTER ONE

All I remember is water, so much water and it feeling so cold, as if I would never be warm again. That was how they got me and my brother; we became were so cold we must have blacked out. The last thing I remember was the darkness as the water covered my head and the voice. His voice telling me to fight. In my mind I saw his eyes, eyes of fire, but they too were drowned out in the cold.

CHAPTER TWO

Amber watched from the window as her baby brother was put into the large black car. He was crying, calling for her, she knew that she should care, she should be going mad, the world should be drenched in red but for one reason or another she couldn't make herself care.

She watched unmoved from the window as the car drove away feeling nothing, numb from the inside out, she knew something was wrong with her but not what. She was so cold and somewhere inside she was screaming, she was sure but that part of her was so small and seemed trapped in ice, it was so easy to just stay numb.

She could watch from a distance but it didn't touch the inside didn't melt the cold ball, which seemed to have taken the place of her emotions. She sat and watched a small part of her took notice of the faces taking her baby brother it tucked away the information, safe in the heat the small flicker of flame still burning in the shield of ice where she couldn't touch.

Blinking she tried to feel something about what was happening but it took too much effort so she went back to just staring out of the window shivering.

Voices where talking behind her, something caught her interest, it told her to listen so she tried for a second to fight the numbness but it took too much effort and she was so cold fighting it just hurt too much. The pain was too much for her to cope with so she let her mind drift, listening but not listening to the voices.

"She will be out of it from now on I promise you just keep the money coming and she will be safe. Her drugs work by keeping her in a dreamlike state she won't care what happens to her brother she won't even care what happens to her."

The voices moved away laughing, she turned her attention to the window again it had started to rain and she watched as the rain made a path down the window. She lifted a hand and traced the path. Sighing, she was about to let her mind drift again when she saw from the corner of her eye a young, thin woman standing next to her. She was watching her, she thought about talking to the girl but that took too much effort yet again so she wrinkled her nose and looked away. That small part of her screamed "this is wrong!" it tried to fight, telling her about the fire and him and her brother but again it slipped away, the thought wiped in a haze that it was just too hard to think but she noticed the thin girl moving closer.

"Hi, you need to listen it's not hard to listen just stop your mind from wandering for a second, they are drugging you, keep listening. I know it's hard but you need to stop taking the drugs, it's hard to connect to you, you're too far away. Find a way to stop taking the drugs."

Before Amber could turn to her she was gone. Drugs, she thought. That would explain a lot, I should stop taking the drugs, she nodded her head but then the thought slipped away and she went back to staring out of the window. I wonder, she thought, as she drifted away on a cloud of nothing, I wonder, who I am? Why am I looking out of this window? Where am I? And why is it so cold in here.

Amber woke to find she was in a room looking out of the small window which was too high up and too small to climb through or open. But it showed her whether it was day or night. She saw it was night, not sure what had woken her and she laid there and listened. There it was again, that fleeting whistling, turning her head towards the door she lay where she was, watching it she could feel her body shivering inside. She felt cold and the small part of herself she could tell was frightened but she couldn't feel the fear. She knew she needed to fear the whistling but she couldn't remember why. Her body and brain kept trying to send her back to sleep and she found she was fighting it but again wasn't sure why the cotton wool in her brain was too big and thick as she turned her head towards the sound. She followed it along the wall till it stopped moving, the whistling was just outside her door now. Closing her eyes she heard the jingling of the keys, someone was coming into her room she opened her eyes to slits fighting the response of her body trying to sleep. She watched the door handle praying that it wouldn't turn and that they would move on, she didn't know who or what was behind the door but the light at the bottom of the door from outside darkened that no-one should be entering her room in the night while she was sleeping. She was a good girl, she was sure she was, frowning she felt the cotton wool was pulling her under to sleep again, and the thoughts were trying to flee, but the feeling of fear the first emotion she had felt in a long time kept her together enough to fight of the cotton wool in her head and she stayed awake as slowly the door handle turned and someone walked in.

They walked up to her bed and looked down at where she lay, She closed her eyes and let the numbness seep in so she was on the edge of nothingness the fear drained away as if it had never been, but for the first time a memory fought through and she remembered what the girl had said stop taking the drugs, fight, so she fought the drug to stay awake inside her the small flame enclosed in ice seemed to glow brighter for a few seconds melting the cold frost inside as she heard whoever it was walk up and looked down at her, she then heard another set of foot treads and another person entered the room stopping at the bottom of her bed.

"We need to dose her again she is due."

"Hurry, make her sit up and take it, we need to make sure they aren't any marks, it's more than my jobs worth if they find needle tracks."

"Fine, she's so doped she will take it straight anyway, she's cute if you know what I mean."

Amber felt the cover lifting from her then she felt a hand moving along over her body and own her legs, before it travelled up then up to touch her breast. She lay still making sure that they thought she was a sleep, But the numbness was fading, Fear was returning and a small fire was starting inside as the fear once again broke through the numbness, as the cover was moved completely off her, she felt the hand moving her legs apart and she wondered if she could still lay still if he kept on touching her, And knew that she couldn't, as she was about to move the other voice stopped him.

"Stop that, we don't have time and we aren't paid to rape her just dope her now, hurry up."

She felt the hand give her breast one harder squeeze, and the other hand leave her legs before the man sighed and whispered,

"Pity, maybe next time I will make time for us."

Laughing he lifted her up and shocked her, calling

"Wake, wake, sleeping beauty pill time, come on you need to take your meds."

Amber pretended to wake and let him place a cup to her mouth, she spilled liquid into her mouth, it was sweet and she wanted to swallow it.

"Open now let me see well done good girl back to sleep with you now."

Amber felt herself being laid down, felt a needle go in her arm. Holding the liquid half way down her throat she waited for both people to moved away, As she lay there she waited till she heard the door shut behind them before pulling the cover off. She sat up and looked around slowly still fighting the drugs in her system, Looking around she looked for somewhere where she could spit the liquid out and found she had a bath room. It was across from her the door was open and she could see the sink in it, sliding out of her bed, she slowly walked across the room using the chest of drawers the only thing in her room as a support on the way to the bathroom once there she spat the liquid out of her mouth and using the taps at the sink she washed the liquid away. Sitting on the toilet edge she took a breath before starting back to the bed laying back down she let the drug remaining in her system to once again take her under.

Amber found herself drifting into reality again, but this time something was different she was again sitting by the window looking out of it but she remembered she had sat there before she felt more normal, the ball of ice was still there but this time it was smaller a fire was melting it, she felt like she could reach out and touch her emotions but there was still something stopping her from letting the feeling out.

She looked out the window once again this time the sun was out and made the grounds bright she saw there was grass over the other side of what looked like a drive, beyond a huge line of trees she could see it disappeared into the distance the drive was wide rounding on itself and disappearing over a small hill at some point she could see it merged into the trees, It was wide enough for two cars to pass each other and there was a large sign at the point where the drive lengthened into the curve she couldn't see what It said as it was facing away from her window, she could see some of the building she was in, It had two sides each had windows it looked like it was three stories high.

Amber turned from the window and studied the room she was in; it was full of other people some who stared into space like she had been. Others were rocking back and forth. While other were staring at a TV screen where an old move was playing. Looking around she found she couldn't see the young woman who had spoken to her a few days ago, least she thought it was a few days since she had listened to the thin woman, if she had listened to a woman, if there was a woman. She hadn't seen her again and all the days were a big blur each rolling into the other. She had found she was getting more alert as time went by since she stopped taking the drugs they gave her in the night, she had worked out that it was every other night they would creep into her room making her take the liquid before injecting her and leaving pretending that they had never been there to begin with. Luckily for her the one who had attempted to rape her hadn't come back yet, she could feel her self-getting stronger, something was waking up in her and she knew she would be ready for him if or when he did try again.

There was something wrong with her she knew that. The staff would look at her from the corner of their eyes and she could smell their fear it was nice it tasted like spices on her tongue, she knew she shouldn't be able to smell their fear or know that tasted of wine on her tongue she didn't even knew how she knew what wine tasted like or why. Her mind would throw that description up to her as she tasted their fear, she knew that she should know what was wrong but as she tried to remember and follow the train of thought she knew she was losing it, the thoughts were slipping like quicksand through her mind she didn't remember, and that should worry her but it didn't, she did wonder why they the nurses and doctors were scared of her but as she thought the thought it was gone like leaves in the wind blown away, turning back to face outside the window she knew with a small part of her mind she there was something about tablets and that she needed to not low the fact that she wasn't taking the tablets to the nurses she was aware at some level that she knew they were scared of her for a reason she had stopped taking the tablets and that stayed in her mind at all times that was enough for the minute. She didn't need to know why that badly at the moment and again like the previous though like dust the thoughts blew away and she was again blank and staring out the window wondering where she was and too tired to care, but a small part stayed awake watching notice and getting more and more stronger and alert.

Three weeks later

Amber watched through her hair which was over her face covering her eyes as the doctors wheeled someone into a room next to hers, she watched quietly it was late and there were only a few of the other people who she had figured out were patents like herself locked up in this place with her, out of their rooms the nurse were letting them stay out as it was Halloween, it was a special treat she watched as the doctor in charge Doc she thought his name was but as he didn't bother her she couldn't retain his name for now, she did remember he was the doctor in charge of the new patent but something had alerted her that this parent was different.

Maybe it was the way the doctors and nurses kept looking around at everyone each time someone looked over to her she lowered her eyes, they still thought that she was spaced out and drugged up she knew that she was getting clearer,but remembered the first night one of the men had said something about needle marks she hadn't thought about that thinking that it was just the tablet she had been fed, but now she was beginning to think the table was what had kept her confused but they were injecting her at night with something as well the tablets, only the tablets had stopped her feeling the pain of the needle going in and liquid had distracted her so she hadn't noticed, now she could feel the needle going in at night could feel whatever was in it helping to confused her so she didn't pay attention to what was happening some of the confusion was going. Her mind clearing slowly, But the barrier of her emotions was still there she still had to fight to pay attention to what was going on she need to think of a way to stop them injecting her. She watched as the person was rolled into the room, his hands were tired down on the bed but that wasn't what had caught her attention, beside the strange way the doc and nurse were behaving it was something about him but she didn't know what. Then it hit her it was his eyes which were locked on her they weren't human he was rolling his head moaning, she watched as his eyes rolled around the room and to her surprise she could sense his panic beneath the drugs they were still pumping into him. Just before he disappeared into the room his eyes locked on to her again and without thinking she looked up letting him see her. He stopped moaning as they locked eyes, and one of the doctors looked up and around she broke eye contact before he could spot her and after a few seconds the man started to moan again the doctor looked down his concentration once again on the man being wheeled into the room where a few seconds later the door was closed and the man was gone.

Amber looked down to where her hands had been laying on the window still there were eight little burn marks where her hands had fisted as they lay on the window looking down at them she put her hands into the pockets of the old grey dressing grown she had on everyone had them. They were like part of the uniform patients were given long dress in a dull blue for the girls and brown jogging bottoms for the boys with an off white dull t shit for the boys, one dull over long to big fitting dressing grown for everyone shaking her head.

Amber moved from the space with the burn marks she had been leaving marks for a few days now and knew that one of the nurse was convinced one of them had a lighter somewhere so she had, had the whole of the room searched and all the rooms on this floor, but had so far found nothing Amber smiled to herself wonder what the nurse would think if Amber showed her it was her making the marks probably dope her up more Amber thought as she made her way to her room.

Lying down on her bed she closed her eyes, tonight was the safe night as she began to think of them. Tonight she would be left alone, last night they had poured the liquid down her throat she had spat it out once they had left but she had noticed last night she was a lot warmer one of them had commented on it. The other had looked worried and decided to check with someone but felt that they should up the dose, looking inside her-self-Amber had seen the fire inside melt the ball of ice it was now a small ball of fire, and with the fire was one thought, small at the moment so she could ignore it, but gowning burn twisting and getting louder "Find then, find them both."

Four weeks later

Lying on her bed she watched as with a thought a small flame danced on her finger tips it didn't burn, but she knew it was hot, the flame was a beautiful blue she watched as it danced and found memory's slowly waking in the flame.

She watched as a small girl played with fire the way one might play with a ball bouncing it and throwing it. There was a tall man there and a beautiful woman she was holding a small baby she was on fire but didn't burn. The flames danced around her as if she was made of fire they were all smiling. Amber fisted the flame in her hand putting it out she knew pain came with that memory but she couldn't feel it, she still wasn't sure what she was but she now knew she wasn't a normal human she could play with fire and the knowledge poured into her that, that was what had gotten her mum and dad killed and her brother who was still alive and god the rage at that thought felt good hot she sipped it each time she remembered while she could hold the thought in her mind it never stayed, the same as the rage something kept stealing them both away. When she remembered him she remembered each time before as if the memories weren't gone just hidden the knowledge of her not being human was why she was taken it was also the reason she was here and why they kept her doped up.

Claire watched the girl from the door way she was playing with fire and Claire knew if she got caught playing with it the game would be up. But it was a good sign it meant she had listened to her and got of the drugs. She had made the right choice in approaching her; she stood watching till the girl looked up then taking a deep breath she smiled.

Amber looked up she saw the thin woman standing by her door watching her smiling.

Amber sat up trying not to frighten her but it was fine the thin woman skipped over to where Amber sat still smiling.

"You're off the confusion drugs. Good."

Amber smiled at the woman

"Yes, thank you "

The thin woman nodded.

"They killed me with their drugs I was in this room as well."

Amber watched as the woman looked around the room as if she was remembering. Amber studied the woman as she looked around she was about twenty with beautiful mahogany skin and long curly hair which seemed to have faded blue high lights, her eyes were green as emerald's but washed out at the same time she was a faded picture of what should have been a strong beautiful woman, she was dressed in a red dress which was also faded but she had bare feet.

"What happened to you if your dead why are you still here?"

Amber thought she had asked the wrong thing as the woman waved fading even more almost disappearing but she seemed to change her mind she waved back into view Smiling she looked at Amber

"I like your hair."

She stretched her hand to Amber's hair as if to touch it her hair had been a dull black but now she had noticed it had a small amount of red streak's running thought, Amber leaned forward to let her touch when it when they both hear a moan coming from one of the walls, Amber straightened back up the man they brought in, Amber thought, his moans got louder the woman shock her head

"They won't like that they only give you two weeks to moan and his been doing it for four weeks."

Amber looked at her

"What the moaning?"

She nodded her head

"The moans don't last long here they don't like it, they stopped you with the tablets."

Walking over to the wall closes to where the sound was coming from her disappeared through the wall and reappeared just as quick. The woman smiled at Amber

"He's different, like you. I did try to tell him but he couldn't see me, too far gone"

Before Amber could ask what she meant the woman stood straight and bent her head to the left before disappearing completely. Leaving Amber alone with the moaning laying down she stared up at the ceiling for a while before letting sleep over take her, tomorrow, she thought tomorrow I start to find a way out of here, and if, she thought opening her eyes turning her head to again stare at the wall where the sound was coming from if, his like me maybe he will have answers as to why they are taking us, I will take him with me and this place will burn and closing her eyes on that thought, she slept.

Out now on Amazon

22687309R00078

Printed in Great Britain
by Amazon